Beaver St

1

CHAPTER ONE

There hadn't been a beaver seen in Beaver City, Oregon for over 50 years, but Brax found one.

Knowing about the beaver was a million dollar secret in his pocket and he wasn't going to spend it. Ever.

Even if he did spend it, that wouldn't stop the other guys from teasing him. It just wouldn't. All the guys in Beaver City played team sports and Brax didn't.

The teasing started the day Brax walked off the T-ball field right in the middle of a game. That was in first grade. Now he was finishing fifth grade and he still didn't like team sports. Sure, he could swing a bat or make a home run as well as most guys his age. He just didn't want to. He was more interested in other things. Like watching the beaver.

Maybe Brax was being too careful. If he were reckless he could spill the whole beaver secret and be popular-for a minute or two. He might even become semi-famous for a discovery like this: a beaver in

Beaver City! It might be posted on one of those nature blogs or be recorded in the town history or something. Beavers returning to Beaver City!

But it was no good. He knew he could keep a secret.

Living in Beaver City was like living in a forest. He loved the bright green ferns, huckleberries, and fir trees. He was accustomed to the brown pine needle carpet and the chocolate colored tree trunks, But the rusty orange teeth were a new sight. When they flashed upstream, he jumped.

Brax moved slowly along the creek, edging his way toward a spot where he'd have a clearer view. He wasn't afraid of the beast attacking him. He knew beavers were herbivores. And they were gentle. If he didn't bother the beaver, the beaver wouldn't bother him. Still, he felt nervous as he approached the dark brown animal.

He saw the webbed feet. The flat tail. The husky body. The orange teeth chomping industriously.

A beaver in Beaver City!

Brax wasn't going to tell anyone. Ever.

But then he met Kate.

CHAPTER TWO

Kate didn't really live in Beaver City. Her parents had dropped her off to stay with her grandparents for the summer while they looked for a new home in California. Kate was going to be a model for a big clothing company there. She was that pretty.

Brax began to fidget at his school desk. Kate had only moved there a month ago and she was already popular. And she didn't even play sports.

"Friends," Mrs. Huddleston announced, "I know it's the last week of school before summer break…"

A loud cheer erupted.

"…And you're thinking we'll probably coast through this last week cleaning out desks and such."

The students giggled agreement.

"But I have a special project for us to do!"

A collective groan rose up from the desks.

"I'm assigning you into teams of two," she continued. "Each team will choose an animal to study, then you'll do a report for the class to complete our last biology unit."

Brax winced. *Teamwork.*

"Kate, since you are our newest friend, we'll start with you. You will be paired up with Braxton."

Brax winced again. A couple of boys snickered. One pointed at him and made a face.

Brax sighed. He got teased a lot. Sometimes bullied. But the only thing worse than not playing sports was whining. He didn't want to be a whiner. That's why he'd never tell Mrs. Huddleston about the teasing. Not ever.

Kate got up and traded seats with the boy next to Brax. The boys snickered again. Mrs. Huddleston continued the pairing of teams.

"Hey Brax." Kate pulled out a notebook and a pencil.

"Hey."

Though Brax had barely talked to Kate before, he knew a lot about her. He studied people the same way he studied animals. Kate wasn't just pretty. She was friendly. She liked everyone. She was smart. She was confident.

But Kate was vain.

"What animal do you want to study?" Kate gathered up her long wheat-colored hair and flipped it over one shoulder. She quickly twisted it into a braid.

Brax wasn't going to tell anyone about the beaver. Not even beautiful, friendly Kate. Not ever.

There were thousands of animals to choose from and there were lots of ways to study them. The internet was filled with animal documentaries. Mrs. Huddleston didn't say they had to actually *observe* one in the wild.

"Well?" Kate poised her pencil over her notebook.

Brax didn't mean to say it. He didn't want to say it. He told himself not to say it.

But he said it.

"Beavers."

CHAPTER THREE

The school bell rang.

Brax snatched up his backpack from the floor and headed straight for the door. He was always the first one out. Always.

Just as he cleared the doorway he glanced over his shoulder. A swarm of students buzzed around Kate. She put on more shiny lip goop. She smiled a perfect-teeth smile. She laughed at something a boy said. A perfect, happy laugh.

Brax unlocked the chain from his bike. He flung his backpack over one shoulder and hopped on. With one foot on the pedal he felt a sudden pull. He jerked backward.

"I see you have a new girlfriend," sneered Lucas. Gabe and Brandon sniggered.

Lucas Freeman was a bully. But he wasn't a noisy, in-your-face bully. Lucas didn't leave bruises or scrapes. He was mean in a polite, civilized way. Brax's dad called it 'passive-aggressive.' Brax called it sneaky.

Brax looked from one boy to the next. They were no bigger than he was. No stronger either. He could beat all of them at pull-ups and push-ups, easy.

"She's not my girlfriend, Lucas. You saw Mrs. Huddleston pair us up."

"I see the way you watch her, Brax. You *like* her!"

Lucas kicked the back tire. Just enough to make Brax grip the handles.

"Looks like your tires could use some air." Lucas ruffled Brax's hair. Slowly, he grabbed a wad and pulled it.

"Well, guess we'll see you at football practice…oh wait…you don't play football!"

The three boys smirked. Brax put his foot on the pedal.

What is the big deal with sports? It's not like it's the only way a guy can prove he's a real guy.

Brax pedaled hard. Maybe the speed would whip the worried thoughts from his mind.

It's not fair. Nobody teases girls if they don't play

sports. Nobody says they aren't enough of a girl if they don't like football. It's not fair. It just isn't.

Brax didn't head straight for home. His parents were both at work and Beaver City wasn't a big city like New York. In Beaver City kids could still wander around. So Brax headed for his million dollar secret place.

The beaver dam was in the perfect spot. Nobody cared about the discarded fields that used to be part of a pro golf course fifty years ago. Giant Douglas fir bordered the edges of the fields as far as he could see. Huge cottonwood and oak trees gathered in unruly clumps everywhere. Jorey Creek wound its way through the whole 153 acres of wilderness.

Sure, kids could wander around a small town like Beaver City, but they rarely wandered here. This was a wild place. A place where the creek ran swift and deep. A place where you could be quiet and sometimes sit for hours watching wild animals. This was no place for *football players.*

Brax smiled.

He could see traces of the old golf course. Big ponds that used to be water challenges for the golfers were now filled with fish and frogs. Wildflowers covered what used to be plateaus for putters.. And a decaying building, almost completely swallowed by blackberry bushes, had once been the pro shop.

But the best leftover was the stone bridge that crossed the deepest part of Jorey creek. The bridge was overgrown. Its gray-green stones were mossy. Mushrooms and fungus grew at the base, and vines of ivy wrapped around the pillars at each end.

The bridge was also special for another reason: it was big enough to conceal a beaver dam underneath.

Brax stowed his bike between the crumbling building and the creek. The banks were slick with a clay-like mud that reminded him of an old cabin. He breathed it in: rotting wood, creek water, weeds, all warm in the early June sun.

Before the golf course, this place was a gravel quarry. The carved out cliffs from the long ago quarry rose up sharply on the south side of the creek. Jorey

Creek called out to the cliffs and the sound echoed back.

This was another world, far away from school projects and bullying. He may have accidentally suggested that he and Kate study beavers for their report, but he would never accidentally tell her about this place. Not ever.

He made his way down the steps wedged into the north side of the creek. They weren't real steps, just big stones he'd found near one of the ponds. He carried them all the way himself, and worked for days to get them all pushed into the creek bank. *I bet football players can't do that.*

Balancing on an overturned log, he walked to the big sitting rock near the base of the bridge. He climbed up the smooth slope of the rock and perched himself on the side closest to the bridge so the beaver wouldn't notice him.

The tidy criss-cross of logs and sticks were still there. The dam looked even larger than the last time. He knew it might be awhile before he saw the beaver so he settled himself in a sunny spot and waited.

He closed his eyes and tilted his face to the sun. Sunshine was a rare commodity in Beaver City and he didn't want to waste a drop of it. As he sat soaking in the golden warmth, his body relaxed and his thoughts wandered.

He thought about Kate.

Kate's parents were moving all the way to California just so she could be a model. She would probably end up famous and make a lot of money. Working with Brax on one dumb school project the last two weeks of school wouldn't matter to her. She wouldn't remember him. He would become just another person on a long list of admirers that she wouldn't look twice at. He would probably see her on the cover of some magazine one day and remember the time she lived in Beaver City.

A sharp snap of branches made his eyes flash open. The beaver was swimming upstream toward the den with a branch in its mouth. Behind the beaver he saw a flash of movement. Something was following.

This beaver was a mother, and two babies were trailing right behind her.

CHAPTER FOUR

The baby beavers followed their mother right up to the entrance of the den. Instead of diving underwater and going inside, the mother beaver climbed up the mound, dragging the tree branch to the top. One baby followed her up onto the heap and snuffled around the branch. The other swam in quiet circles.

Brax knew where the entrance was even though it was below the creek surface. He had seen the beaver dive under right there many times.

Three beavers in Beaver City.

The baby on top of the den had the same coloring as its mother: golden brown fur, black nose and ears, and shining black bead-like eyes. The baby mimicked its mother's movements—pushing the branch with its tiny brown claws.

He thinks he's helping. Brax nearly laughed out loud. Luckily, he caught himself in time.

The other baby, currently swimming in circles, was different. It was gray with whitish jowls and chin. Its funny mouth looked like a smile.

There was a splash as the mother slid down off the heap and landed in the water. The helpful baby followed her while the playful one swam in loopy patterns, sending smooth ripples across the water.

As the mother and her golden baby started to swim downstream, Brax heard a soft bark. The gray baby twitched its nose and answered its mother's call with a muffled honk. Then it followed her downstream.

Brax leaned forward and watched the three beavers swim. They moved as smoothly as seals. He was mesmerized.

Is there a dad for this beaver family? How big can beavers get? Why are their teeth orange? What would they do if they knew I was here?

The mother made her way to the side of the creek and pulled at some weeds. She wadded the green mass into a ball and chewed it. Her babies tried to claw at her green wad but she stuffed it into her mouth and pulled at some more. The babies mimicked her. Soon they were eating tiny wads of the bright green pond weed.

They look like big hamsters.

After eating their fill, the beavers swam back toward the den. Brax held his breath as they came closer. The mother dived under and the first baby followed her. The second baby looked right up at Brax before quietly dipping out of sight.

He looked right at me! He knows I'm here and he didn't even look scared!

He didn't really know if the beaver was a he or a she, but it didn't matter. He felt like he had just made a new friend.

He waited another twenty minutes, but the beavers didn't come out. The shadows across the creek told him it was late, so he quietly slid down the rock and crept up the muddy stone.

He wished he had his phone with him so he could have taken pictures.. His parents gave him a phone but he didn't like to carry it around. His phone held a lot of personal information—pictures, texts, and all kinds of science apps that the guys at school would make fun of if they ever got hold of it.

A phone is too personal of a thing. He wasn't going to take his to school or anywhere.

Besides, he wasn't sure he wanted any evidence of this million dollar secret. What if it got out? Lots of people got into trouble from things on their phones. That wasn't going to be him.

He wasn't going to cause any trouble for these beavers. Not ever.

CHAPTER FIVE

Lucas sat on the edge of Brax's desk, tossing a football into the air—and flirting with Kate.

When he saw Brax come into the room he narrowed his eyes and reached down to flick one of Kate's golden braids. Kate's laugh was as golden as her hair. Playfully, she slapped at Lucas.

"So, you and Kate are studying beavers." Lucas turned his back so Kate couldn't see. He flashed his front teeth at Brax in a beaverish grin.

Brax shouldered past him and plopped down in his seat, dropping his backpack to the floor.

"Hi Brax." Kate smiled at him, showing her bright, white, perfectly even teeth. Lucas tossed the football across the room to Gabe and found his own seat.

"Why did you have to tell Lucas about the beavers?" Brax demanded.

"I didn't know it was a secret," she answered sweetly. "He told me that he and Charlene are studying sharks."

Lucas would choose an animal like a shark. It rips living things apart.

"I hear there's a football game after school today. Do you play?"

Brax wasn't sure if Kate was really asking him or if Lucas had already told her and she was just rubbing it in. He exhaled a tired breath. "No."

Kate gently bumped him with her shoulder. "It's ok. I don't *support* football. My grandmother says it's *dangerous*."

Was Kate saying he didn't do dangerous things? Was she calling him weak, afraid, a wuss?!

"I do much more dangerous things than play football." He frowned at Kate.

"Oh no, I didn't mean that. It's just all that brain damage that can happen when people play football. My grandmother knows because she does *research.*" Kate said this last word importantly.

"Dive right into your project," Mrs. Huddleston instructed."You'll need to use every minute of this class if you want to finish in time."

A buzz of voices filled the air as students opened laptops and pulled books from the biology shelves. Kate reached into an expensive looking leather bag and pulled out a piece of paper.

"I put together a short list of resources for us to start with." She pushed the paper across the desk toward him. "Don't worry, I'm not a control freak who has to do things my way." She laughed. He liked the smooth honey sound in that laugh.

He read through the list. Kate had done her homework. There were websites, video links, blogs, and a few book titles.

"Did you know that a beaver hasn't been seen here in Beaver City for a really long time?" Kate pointed to the bottom of the list. Her finger rested on a website link for the Beaver City historical society.

"Yeah, I knew that." Brax shrugged, trying to sound disinterested. He didn't want to be that guy who knew too much about beavers, or any other animal.

"Well, I think it's cool that you know so much about

beavers. My grandmother says that people should be more interested in the planet." Kate smiled her honey smile. Her lip gloss glinted in the light coming in from the window.

He wasn't sure if Kate really believed that or if she was just trying to be nice. Anyway, it wouldn't work. He wasn't about to open up to her about his interests even if she was really pretty, really smart, and really nice. *Not gonna happen.*

Lucas wandered over. He sat on the edge of the desk and ran his hand through his thick hair.

"Hey, did you know that beavers eat trees?"

Kate was busily writing notes with her colored gel pen.She didn't even look up as she corrected him.

"Actually, they don't really eat trees. They strip away the bark from trees and eat the softer stuff underneath. And they only do that in the winter when there's less food around."

Brax couldn't help it. He laughed. Lucas snapped his head around to glare at him. Then he smiled a smile that hid a thousand punches.

"See you in the *bleachers*, science boy." Lucas gave the desk a slight shove as he walked back to his own.

Kate raised her face to look at Brax through her silky lashes. She tapped her head a few times and winked.

Ok, maybe he would open up to Kate just a little bit.

Maybe.

CHAPTER SIX

Brax liked being an only child. He liked his parents, he liked their home, and he liked living in Beaver City.

Most of the time.

Beaver City was a small town and the social life of the residents revolved around two things: beer and football.

Fields of hops, plants and flowers used to make beer, fringed the town, so the farmers grew the best hops in Oregon. Every September, people came from all over for the Beaver City beer festival. Brax didn't mind that. Beer smelled good, even if he was too young to drink it now. . Of course, his parents didn't drink it, because they were really *careful* about what they ate and drank. So careful that it annoyed him sometimes.

Then there was football. Lots of football. And not just during football season. There was pee wee football, junior varsity, varsity, and even the Old Guys football team.

Brax liked to watch some of the games his parents took him to, but he thought there was too much football in Beaver City. Way too much for such a small town.

He preferred canoeing. It wasn't exactly a sport in the traditional sense. But it took a lot of strength and special skills. He'd been canoeing when he first spotted what looked like a beaver lodge.

It was only his second time in a canoe. His dad sat in the front, with his mom doing most of the steering in the back. Brax was slumped on a sagging canvas seat in the middle of the canoe. As they floated along on the small lake, his dad snapped photos of everything. Brax laughed as his mom suggested his dad did less snapping and more rowing.

While his parents discussed the good old days of "when we were young," Brax spotted it: not really a lodge, but maybe the beginnings of a small den. Just a pile of sticks really. The sticks didn't look like something the river had just left there. They looked like they had been placed there. *Organized.*

He wanted to shout, to tell his parents about his discovery. But for some reason, he didn't. Maybe this discovery was a random pile of sticks. But maybe not.

His dad told Brax to take the front seat and practice paddling. Brax loved the smooth resistance of the water against his paddle when he pushed the paddle deeper. The water felt thick, almost like it wasn't water at all. He liked the powerful forward movement that each stroke created as he dug in, ran the paddle along the side of the boat, then quickly flipped it out of the water behind him. He felt his muscles strain and burn as he paddled faster and harder. The boat skimmed the surface quietly, gracefully, with only the gentle splash of the paddles breaking the silence.

The pile of sticks turned out to be nothing but a pile of sticks. But it put him on the lookout for beavers. When he found a real beaver lodge, he knew what it was right away.

Now, he was glad that the first sighting was just a pile of sticks. If it had been a real beaver dam, then everyone in town would have come to see it. Who knew what would happen to the beavers then?

The real beaver lodge was in a safe spot. A hidden spot. A spot no one would find.

Brax trusted his parents, but he wasn't going to tell them about his million dollar secret. At least, not yet.

It was tempting to tell. Making a discovery like that could win him some respect. Maybe the guys at school would quit teasing him about football. Well, Lucas probably wouldn't..

But having a secret made him feel special. Smart.

Kate liked smart people. People who knew things about the planet.

When he thought about Kate, he was tempted to share the secret. The temptation was as powerful as the stroke of a canoe paddle in the water.

But Brax wasn't just strong on the outside, he was strong on the inside. He could keep a secret, and he could keep it forever.

CHAPTER SEVEN

Brax took binoculars with him.

This time he wanted to see the beavers up close.

As he sat on the large boulder the rain misted down on his head and shoulders. He was glad he had stuffed his hoodie in his backpack. Weather in Oregon was unpredictable.

As he waited for the beavers to come out of the den, he thought about that afternoon's research with Kate.

They learned why beavers' front teeth were rusty orange colored. They also learned that the ecosystem wouldn't survive long without beavers and the work they did. Kate found some really great videos online of beaver calls. Together they printed up pictures of beavers and their lodges. Kate even edited one of the photos so the beavers in the picture looked like they were holding up mugs of foamy beer.

Kate told him about the dance lessons, photo sessions, clothing fittings, and special diet she had to be on just to be a teen model. It seemed her life revolved around the way she looked. Brax was surprised she had time for anything else.

When she adjusted her braid and glossed her lips for the millionth time that day, Brax asked a bold question.

"Don't you ever get tired of worrying about the way you have to look?"

"The *way I have to look?*" Kate's perfect face frowned for the first time.

"I mean, it's cool that you'll be a famous model and everything." Brax stumbled. "But don't you get kinda sick of having to be always on...*display?*"

Kate didn't answer. She turned back to the keyboard. "Do you know that beavers use their big flat tails to slap the water as a warning?" Her face looked casual, but her voice squeaked a little.

Oh crap. Opening up is a bad idea.

Brax heard a splash as the last beaver flipped to the surface of the water. He hadn't even noticed the beavers emerge. Now, they were already heading downstream. He snatched up the binoculars and focused on the baby swimming at the back of the watery trail.

The binoculars were old but still good. He always had a difficult time getting the lenses to focus. He closed one eye and slowly turned the dial. Then he closed the other eye and did the same. By the time he got the binoculars focused, the beavers were further downstream.

He held the black field glasses tight against his face and desperately scanned the creek. With the glasses still up to his eyes, he stepped forward.

The mossy rock was slippery after the misty rain. That one step was all it took.

He hit the rock hard, slid down its curved edge, and with his legs scraping against boulders, he plunged into the water.

CHAPTER EIGHT

The cold creek water swirled into his nostrils and filled his ears. The shock of it caused his hands to ball into fists and his legs to curl up near his body.

But he wasn't going to panic. He bobbed to the top and gasped for air, spitting out the murky fluid. The current was strong, stronger than it looked from the top of the boulder. He felt its power surround him and pull him in every direction. The water wasn't calm like at the surface. This water yanked and twisted and shoved. It swirled like a liquid tornado and tried to pull him under.

He felt the panic start in his gut and rise up to his throat. He remembered his dad telling him that panic was every man's first mistake. Taking a huge breath of air, he forced himself to paddle against the strong current toward the muddy bank.

Brax was a good swimmer. But even with his solid strokes, the pull from the water was strong. He tried to quell his panic by keeping his eyes on the creek bank.

When he neared the edge he put his feet down but found only rocks slick with moss. He tried to stand but slipped back into the water again, this time banging his knees hard on the large river rocks underneath. The current snatched him and dragged him a few yards downstream. Some grasses in the water swished against his legs, making him cry out in surprise. He flailed his arms and kicked his legs, writhing away from the slithery grasses.

He knew he needed to calm down and make a plan quick. He looked downstream and caught sight of a huge tree near the water's edge.He stopped flailing and waited for the water to carry him toward the tree. When he neared the tree, he gave one big push, lunged at an overhanging branch, and caught hold. The gnarly branch tore at his hands, but he held tight. He pulled himself up out of the water an inch at a time and moved his bloodied palms along the length of the branch. Warm sweat mingled with the cold water soaking him through. Near the bank, he looked for a clear spot but found only thick shrubs. Instead of dropping he inched toward the trunk of the tree, the weight of his soaked clothes pulling him down.

As he approached the trunk he realized it was too large—he'd never get his arms around it. Beneath him was a huckleberry bush. He let go.

The thin branches snapped as he fell, and the unripe berries patterred to the ground. The damp woodsy air filled his lungs. He lay still, trying to figure out if any part of him was broken. Finally, he sat up, untangled himself from the brittle branches, and crawled out of the tattered bush up the creek bank.

His clothes were sodden and muddy, his knees were bruised, and his hands were torn and bleeding. He looked upstream to the boulder he had slipped from and saw the binoculars, still perched on the boulder's edge just above the water.

That could have been the last thing I ever did. Look through those glasses at the beavers.

He shuddered. Then relief washed over him. He felt like crying. And laughing.

He trudged along the riverbank. The beavers were

gone. His fall probably scared them off. He picked up his backpack and the old spy-glasses as he passed the boulder. Then he climbed the step stones and headed toward home.

He wanted to be cleaned up before his parents came home. He wasn't ready to explain where he'd been and what he'd been doing. Not yet.

Passing through a community park, Brax noticed a poster taped to a message board near the drinking fountain.

Beaver City Town Meeting

Developers Rand & Port desire to purchase the old golf course land parcel for housing developments.

His muscles tightened. The old golf course land? The wilderness he loved to explore?

Come make your voice heard. Open forum.

Open forum?

He wasn't sure what that meant, but he *was* sure he didn't want to see the old golf course turned into more housing. More housing meant more streets, more cars, more people, more noise. Right near the creek. Right near the beavers. *His* beavers.

Brax ran for home.

CHAPTER NINE

It wouldn't be difficult for anyone who saw Brax's bedroom to figure out what he loved best.

His walls were lined with posters of beautiful, exotic animals. His desk was littered with bird nests, shells, and rocks he'd collected. His windowsill held paper cups filled with seedlings, and a small, rusty watering can sat on the floor nearby. Feathers, a snake skin, a pile of dried rosemary branches and a magnifying glass cluttered the nightstand next to his bed. It was clear that Brax loved the planet.

Sadly, being a planet geek didn't make him popular at school. Not in Beaver City, anyway. Football was popular. Beer was popular. Planet geeking was not.

Even so, he had a couple of friends who shared his love of all things wild. Micah wanted to be a biologist when he grew up and Brodie was interested in paleontology. But those guys were older than Brax and went to a different school, so he only saw them on weekends and holidays.

It would be nice to have close friends in his grade. Although he never felt lonely when he was out exploring fields and streams, he often felt lonely at school.

He quickly showered, put his wet clothes in the washer, and set his soaked shoes on the floor vent to dry. As he toweled his damp hair, he heard his parents open the front door.

Now he had an important task to accomplish: get information from his parents about the town meeting without raising their suspicions.

He sat down at the table for dinner and started to formulate a plan. His dad walked in carrying a basket of just-baked rolls.

"Hey sweetie, did you read about the town meeting tonight?"

"I did," answered Brax's mom. "The big developers who tore out those wetlands and built a senior center now want to get their hands on the old golf course land. I absolutely cannot believe the judge agreed to let them build on those wetlands. Such a shame."

"Well, we really did need a new senior center," his dad replied, "but you're right about the wetlands. Beaver City needs new leadership, people who have preservation in mind."

Brax took a mouthful of the herbed pasta. His mom was a really good cook. He quickly swallowed and brought up his burning question.

"I saw a poster about the town meeting. What does 'open forum' mean?"

His mother scooped up some salad and heaped it on Brax's plate. "It means that community members can come and be a part of the discussion. The town leaders want to know what we all think."

"Does the town want to know what kids think?" He casually speared a cherry tomato with his fork, trying not to look too interested in the answer.

"I don't know if there's an age limit. Some city leaders take children seriously and some don't. Sometimes even the adults aren't listened to. Are you interested in going to this town meeting, Brax?"

There it was. The question. If he answered too hastily, it might open the door of suspicions. He could lie. But he didn't like lying to people, especially when they were his parents."

He snatched up another roll and spread butter on it. He bit off a large mouthful.

"I just want to see what a town meeting looks like," he said between bites of the bread. "You guys are always talking about 'community involvement' and I, uh, just want to see what you're talking about."

He reached for the honey jar that sat on a tray in the middle of the table and drizzled honey onto his roll. He drizzled that honey as casually as he knew how, deliberately coating his fingers with the glistening syrup.

"I'm glad to hear that," his dad responded. "How about the three of us go together, make it a family project?"

Brax sighed relief and licked the honey from his fingers. Mission accomplished. His parents didn't suspect a thing.

CHAPTER TEN

Brax was hoping to see only a handful of old people who used to play golf in the glory days. Old people wouldn't be walking in the wilds and snooping around near Jorey Creek. Old people wouldn't be looking for beavers, and even if they found them, they wouldn't announce it to everyone. Old people weren't looking for attention. They weren't looking for a million dollar secret.

But the room wasn't filled with a handful of older people.

Everybody was there.

There were middle-aged people, young parents, and even a couple of high school groups. Brax saw neighbors and families he knew.

Do all these people know about the old golf course? Do any of them know about the beavers?!

And then he saw Kate.

She sat with her grandparents in a row of chairs near the back of the room. Brax watched her reach into the small cross-body bag hanging from the back of her chair. She pulled out a tube of lip gloss and swiped the tube across her lips before running her hand through her golden hair. Brax snorted. *Why is she always worrying about how she looks?!*

He moved a little closer to where Kate was sitting. He could see a book on her lap. A book about beavers. His heart sped up.

Did Kate know about the beavers?

Brax and his parents found a seat near Kate as the meeting began. She looked over at him and waved. He gave her a limp wave in return. She lifted the book to show him, then winked and put it back in her lap.

Oh, she brought the book to study for our project! He relaxed.

The meeting was boring. Numbers, dates, people's names, and golf course figures swirled in his head. Kate was bent over her book.

Then, suddenly, everyone got louder. Brax perked up. The room was crowded and warm.

People were queuing up for turns to speak into a

microphone. His mother patted his leg and got up to speak. He shifted uncomfortably in his seat.

Please don't say anything about us, about me. His mother got up to the microphone.

"Ok, we know you want to develop the land and we know you have the money to do it." She looked at a man in a charcoal colored suit. "But have you done any research about the plants and wildlife that reside there? Are there any endangered species? Have you had an environmental impact study completed?"

Research? Studies? On his beaver-land?

Brax felt his head swim and his temperature rise. He looked over at Kate. She had closed her book and was listening intently. The crowd of people rumbled with frustration. Finally, the man in the suit had to stand and wave his arms in the air to stop the noise.

"Calm down, calm down!" he yelled above the shouting. "We've done the studies and there aren't any endangered species there. No special owls, no rare butterflies, no dwindling salamanders. There aren't even many deer or coyotes left in those woods.

The animals that *are* left will move on." The man pulled out some papers from a file on his chair. "We have the reports, we've been cleared for development!" He lifted the papers high above his head, as if trying to save them from a pack of ravenous wolves.

"Just because you're a rich developer doesn't mean you can always have your way," said an older woman one row ahead of Brax. He recognized her as the city librarian. "You have to get the City Council to agree to this too. I can tell you, you'll have a fight on your hands."

The meeting soon ended, with a promise to hold another one in a month's time. Brax turned to his dad.

"Another meeting in a month? Does that mean they can't build anything on the land yet?"

"No, they can't. Not yet. A month isn't much time to gather new evidence though." His dad leaned back in his chair and stretched his legs.

"Evidence? For what?"

"Most of the people here would like to keep the

green space free of development," his father explained. "There aren't many open spaces left in or even near Beaver City. People like a little breathing room."

"What could stop them from building there? What kind of evidence would we need to stop them?"

"Well, it would certainly help if we could find an endangered species there, or even a keystone species would be a great find."

"Keystone?"

"A species that plays an important role in the biodiversity of a particular environment." His dad stood up slowly. "Let's head for home, I have to be up early tomorrow morning for a work meeting."

"Dad…" Brax hesitated. "If there's a *keystone* species living on the old golf course land, what will happen to it if the land gets built on? Where will the animals go?"

"Hard to say." They walked through the thinning crowd toward the door. "I know that animals can adapt and move on, but open spaces are disappearing in every community."

Even though the air in the room was stifling, Brax shivered. Learning about the beavers had been exciting because there weren't any more beavers around Beaver City. Watching the beavers had become his favorite thing to do. But now the beavers' lives were being threatened.

As he neared the door, Kate hurried up behind him and nudged him in the back with her book.

"I had an idea during the meeting," she said in a near-whisper. "Meet me after school tomorrow by the bike rack and I'll tell you."

They shuffled through the narrow doorway.

"Is it an idea for our project?" Brax pointed to the book in her hands.

"It's about the golf course land." .

He stopped walking and faced her.

"Why should you care about what happens to the golf course land? You don't even really live here. After summer's over you won't even see Beaver City again."

He really meant she wouldn't see *him* again, but he wasn't about to say that.

"I don't really care what happens to the golf course land," Kate flicked her hair over her shoulder. She glanced at her passing reflection in a window. "But I know *you do*."

Brax stiffened. He felt a stream of perspiration trickle down the center of his back.

"How do you know?"

"Because," Kate skipped ahead of him. "I followed you."

CHAPTER ELEVEN

Brax was furious.

He caught up to Kate. He grabbed hold of her elbow and pulled her to a stop.

"You followed me? Where did you follow me to?! When?!"

Kate glanced at her reflection in a car window. She fingered her hair.

"Yesterday. After school. I followed you to that bridge." She reached into her bag for more lip gloss. Brax snatched the bag from her hands.

"Stop worrying about what you look like! Nobody's looking at you! Nobody cares!" As soon as he said it he wished he hadn't.

Kate glared at him. She slowly reached for the bag.

"You may not have to think about what you look like because you spend most of your time sitting in the wilderness *watching* things. I *have* to care."

"Why did you follow me?" Brax persisted.

"I...was just curious." Kate blushed as she slung her bag over her shoulder. "I knew you didn't go to any games or practices after school, so I wanted to see where you went."

Embarrassment replaced his anger. While he was watching the beavers, Kate had been watching *him.*

"Don't worry, I won't tell anyone at school. You take enough abuse as it is." Kate smiled and nudged him with her shoulder. Brax looked around. No one was near them. No one could hear.

"So, you won't tell anyone about the beavers?"

Kate stopped walking and dropped her voice.

"You found *beavers*?"

He wanted to kick himself. She hadn't even seen them. She didn't know what it was he'd been watching. Now it was too late.

"Crap!" he kicked his toe at a nearby car tire.

"This is perfect!" Kate exclaimed. "We can use them in our project!"

"No!" Brax almost yelled. "No, no we can't. We can't let anyone know they're there." His words tumbled out anxiously. "If people find out about the beavers there will be stupid kids trying to pet them and lame adults trying to photograph them and scientists wanting to study them. There hasn't been a beaver seen in Beaver City…."

"…for a very long time. I know." Kate waved in answer to her grandparents calling her from across the parking lot. "Like I said, let's meet tomorrow and I'll tell you about my idea." She hurried over to her grandparents' car, giving Brax a final wave before going inside.

Brax felt the million dollars drop out of the hole in his pocket. The hole he had put there with his big mouth.

So much for keeping a secret.

CHAPTER TWELVE

Brax didn't fall asleep right away.

His brain wouldn't quiet down and turn off. He closed his eyes and counted backward from 100. But he kept getting to 93 and thinking about Kate, or the beavers, or the new housing development. Then he would start over at 100 again.

If Kate hadn't moved into Beaver City, he wouldn't be her project partner. She wouldn't have followed him to the creek. Only *he* would know about the beavers.

This was a mess. A big mess.

He was so tired. He didn't want to think about all of this right now. . He wanted to sleep. But his brain said no.

A light breeze blew in from behind the old white shutters that framed his window. He heard an owl hooting nearby. Living in Beaver City used to be cool. Now it was complicated.

He closed his eyes and started the countdown

again. The next thing he knew, it was morning.

When he walked into the classroom he saw Lucas and Gabe talking to a group of girls. Brandon tossed a football to Lucas who tried to look casual, like he could catch it in his sleep. He flexed his arm and was about to toss it back when Mrs. Huddleston came up behind him and took the ball.

"Save it for the field, boys. There are two days left to prepare before you make your presentations. Let's get busy."

Lucas winked at the girls and sauntered back to his seat.

He thinks every girl likes him. But some girls are smarter than that. Brax looked around the room for Kate, but she wasn't there.

They were supposed to meet right after school and now she hadn't even come. He didn't mind doing the research on his own, but he was worried about the beavers and what Kate might do. He almost asked Mrs. Huddleston where Kate was, but he didn't want to raise suspicions.

He pulled out the sheet of paper Kate had given him. Her notes were tidy and thorough. He looked down the list and checked off the sources they'd already researched.

He found the computer with their file on it. As he opened up the file, a picture of a beaver standing on a flattened football was the first thing he saw. Kate made that for him. He smiled as he took the laptop back to his desk.

"Brax, Kate will be late this morning, so you'll have to work alone," Mrs. Huddleston told him.

"Is she…sick?" Brax ventured.

"No, no, she's fine. It's a family matter. Keep working on your own for now."

Lucas had been listening in and strolled over. He sat on the edge of the desk, looked around the room, then closed the laptop Brax was typing on.

"What do you want, *Lucas*?" Brax tried to say his name with as much contempt as he could.

"Oh, not a thing, *Braxy*," Lucas sneered. "I see that your girlfriend isn't here. Be sure you don't *cry* about it. You wouldn't want to look like a *wuss*. Oh…wait, you already do!"

He poked Brax in the arm and made a squelching sound in his cheeks. Then he opened the laptop, pushed it closer to Brax, and patted him on the head. "Good work, Brax," he said with manufactured sincerity. He strolled back to his own desk, smiling at the teacher as he went.

Passive aggressive. Lucas is a quiet bully. Sometimes I'd like to quietly trip him and watch him fall flat on his face.

By lunchtime, Kate still hadn't shown up for school. Brax took his sack lunch and sat in his usual spot at a table near the door. A couple of guys from another fifth grade class sat by him, all eating their lunches in silence. As he took the last bite of the sweet apple and got up to leave, one of the other boys spoke.

"Science club is meeting this Saturday morning, in case you're still interested."

"*Still* interested? I've always been interested," Brax

tossed his sack in the trash can.

"I just meant that since you've been hanging out with that new girl, you might not be so interested in science."

"We don't *hang out*. We're just study partners. That's all!"

He pushed open the door and it banged against the wall. The heat rushed to his face. He lowered his gaze to the pavement and nearly bumped into Kate.

"Sorry I couldn't help you this morning, I had a meeting with my agent. She flew up here from California and I couldn't avoid it." Kate flicked her long braid over her shoulder and grabbed him by the arm. "I have an idea." She pulled him to a nearby bench on the edge of the playfield.

"So that developer guy said the studies they did showed there were no endangered animals on the old golf course land. And you don't want anyone to know about the beavers so we can't use them to protect the space."

"What's your point?!" Brax wished his voice didn't

sound so annoyed, but sitting on a bench with Kate wasn't going to stop the rumors about him giving up science for a *girl.*

"My point is…" Kate said the words with deliberate patience. "…we may not have to use an animal to get the land protected. We could use an *artifact.*"

A group of girls walked past. They looked at Brax and giggled. His face flushed for the second time that day.

"An artifact. Like what? Indian arrowheads?" He laughed, forgetting his embarrassment.

"*Native American*," Kate corrected him. "And yes, that's what I meant."

He narrowed his eyes. He didn't want to say anything mean. But…*arrowheads?*

"Kate, I've never heard of anyone digging up any kind of artifacts in Beaver City. Not to mention arrowheads."

He waited for a shadow to cross her face, but it didn't. Instead, she grinned.

"They're about to." The bell rang. They jumped up

and headed back into the classroom.

CHAPTER THIRTEEN

There was no time to ask Kate what she meant. Mrs. Huddleston directed them to take their seats.

"Please have your research information really solid by the end of today. Presentations will begin tomorrow." Their teacher clapped her hands together excitedly and the class buzzed with anticipation.

As the students shifted seats to work with their partners, Lucas intercepted Kate.

"Too bad we couldn't choose our own partners," he said as he reached out to flick her braid.

"Wouldn't have made any difference for me at all." Kate moved away and slipped into the seat next to Brax. She smiled at Lucas. "Good luck with your presentation." Lucas huffed and headed back to his seat.

Brax blushed as he opened up the laptop and searched for their project file.

"Two more days of school and then summer," Kate breathed. "And now we have a summer adventure ahead of us!"

"What are you talking about? What adventure?" Brax shifted in his chair.

"Saving the old golf course land and saving your beavers. It's going to be a *beaver summer*."

Kate put her hand on his and gave it a squeeze.

Brax nervously eyed the room. Kate laughed.

A beaver summer with Kate.

CHAPTER FOURTEEN

"Take me there."

Kate was standing beside Brax as he unlocked his bicycle.

"How do you know I'm going *there*?" Brax fumbled with the lock, then stuffed it hurriedly into his backpack.

"I just know." She flung her leg over the bike and sat down on the cargo rack just behind the seat. "This bike can hold both of us, can't it?"

"People are going to *talk*," Brax whispered without looking up from his pedals.

"Look Brax, you shouldn't care what other people think," Kate scolded as she adjusted her weight. Brax sighed and pedaled away from the school parking lot.

"*You* care," he objected, "you care way too much about what you look like. You DO care what people think."

"I care about how I look because I have to, not because I'm worried that people won't like me. You worry about what people think of you because you want their *approval*."

Brax pedaled harder. *She doesn't know everything.*

Kate held on to Brax's shoulders as they bounced down a grassy slope. At the bottom they leveled off to a dry, weedy field. Brax had to navigate through a tumble of rocks and holes made by ground squirrels. The pedaling and balancing was tricky with a second person on board. The dust of old weed heads powdered their legs and the occasional snake made Kate squeal.

"What did you mean about finding artifacts?" Brax asked as they left the squirrel minefield behind.

"I'll show you when we get there, it's a great idea." Kate sang a song while they weaved in and out of pine trees. Her happy voice sounded muffled in the woods.

"When we get there, we'll need to be quiet," Brax instructed. "The beavers probably won't come out of their lodge if they hear us coming."

Suddenly he realized he didn't mind sharing the million dollars. As long as he could share it with Kate.

He stood up on the pedals to leverage his weight. They bumped up the old stone bridge to the top. Kate hopped off.

"This is beautiful!" she whispered. She took out her cell phone and snapped a few photos. Brax tiptoed to the bridge rail.

Without a word he motioned to Kate. He pointed to a spot below them.

"That's it?" He could hear the disappointment in her voice. "That little pile of branches?"

He nearly sputtered with laughter when he saw what she was pointing at. A small pile of dead branches had accumulated near a rock directly under them. The pile was barely bigger than a football.

"Not *that*..." he corrected her. "*That.*"

He pointed at the beaver den. It was a large mound, carefully constructed with branches woven like cloth. The center piled high and the sides sloped down to where they touched the water. Just downstream of the den, a line of thick branches diverted and dammed the water's flow.

When will they come out? Kate mouthed the words silently.

Brax smiled. He could see the excitement on her face. He motioned for her to follow him off the bridge and down onto the big boulder.

As they sat on the boulder Kate insisted on taking pictures of the two of them. She leaned close to him and smiled. After taking several photos, she handed the phone to him.

"Wait…" he said as she scrolled through the pictures. "Go back."

Kate thumbed back to the first photo.

"Zoom in."

She enlarged the picture.

In the distance, behind the image of Kate and Brax, were three dark, blurry objects in the water.

"Beavers."

Kate spun around.

"They're adorable!" she rasped.

Brax smiled. He knew his million dollar secret was safe.

Kate silently took photos of the family swimming upstream toward them. The beavers seemed to move effortlessly against the current. When they reached a reedy patch of greens, the mother tore at the grass with her massive rusty teeth. The babies followed her example and snatched at the long green plants that swayed near the water's edge.

"The babies don't have orange teeth," Kate whispered. "They must be pretty young."

Brax drew his knees up to his chest and rested his chin on them. He settled in to doing what he did best: observing.

"I see why you like this so much," Kate nudged him with her elbow.

"It's another world. *Their* world."

"Without beavers we'd all be dead." Kate scrolled through the pictures on her phone.

"That's a little dramatic."

"No, it's *fact*. The kind of biodiversity we get from

beavers is amazing. They create water worlds where animals can find food and get water to drink, then larger animals eat those animals and up the food chain you go!"

Lucas had said girls didn't like science geeks like Brax. Science geeks like Brax. Kate not only liked science geeks, she appeared to be one.

Brax studied her for a moment. "I think you need more lip gloss."

She checked her reflection in her phone. "You're terrible."

CHAPTER FIFTEEN

Brax savored the look on Lucas' face when Mrs Huddleston declared his and Kate's presentation one of the very best.

Lucas held a plastic shark while his partner did all the speaking for theirs.

Lame. Lucas does none of the work but keeps his rep. Just because of football.

After the final presentation the class cheered. School was out for the summer!

Most students jostled out of the room, but some lingered to sign yearbooks. Lucas blocked the doorway as Kate was heading out.

"I'll bet you have some *fun plans* for the summer...."

"Yes." Kate smiled warmly. She pushed past him down the hall and out the double doors.

"It doesn't work on *everyone*," Brax said as he scooped up his backpack.

"Don't be jealous, Braxy. Girls just don't like

helpless science geeks. It's not your fault."

Lucas grabbed his football from under his desk and threw it right at Brax's head. The force knocked Brax backward. He stumbled over a chair and hit the floor hard. A group of girls eyed the commotion, then whispered anxiously.

"No teacher and no security camera," Lucas sneered. "And *they* wouldn't say a thing." He nodded at the group of girls and winked. Then he retrieved the ball and laughed.

Brax jumped to his feet even though his head throbbed.. He wasn't going to let the girls or Lucas think he was injured. A couple of bruised legs and scuffed elbows were nothing he couldn't handle.

"At least science *does something* for the world. Football just causes head injuries."

Brax knew it was a stupid thing to say. Provoking Lucas was not a good idea. Brax was afraid of what Lucas might do but at that moment he didn't care. Lucas had it coming.

Lucas held the football in his left hand and

pounded it with his right. He stepped toward Brax slowly, each footstep making Brax's heart beat faster..

Brax steeled himself. He dropped his backpack and tightened his fists.

Go for the nose. The nose hurts.

Just then there was a sharp rap on the window. It was Kate. She smiled her honey smile at Lucas, motioned for Brax to join her, and innocently glanced from one boy to the next.

Thank you Kate!

Though he was relieved, Brax tried to look disappointed. Lucas grunted disgust.

"Saved by a *girl.*"

Brax lifted his backpack to his shoulder and headed outside.

"What was that all about?" Kate had brought her own bicycle and was pulling it from the rack.

"Just Lucas being Lucas."

As they mounted their bikes and pulled out of the school parking lot, Kate reminded Brax of her plan.

"You still haven't asked me about the artifacts,"

she said as they peddled faster.

Brax shook his head doubtfully. "So...what's your plan?"

Once out of view of the school, Kate skid her bike to a dusty stop.

She reached into her bag and pulled out a cloth pouch tied with string. Brax sidled up next to her.

"Check this out." Kate unwrapped what looked like broken pottery and a handful of arrowheads.

"Uh huh." He ran his finger through the pile of shards. "What are you going to do with them?"

"I figured if we put these artifacts on the land the developers want, they'll have to change their plans to build. They can't build on a tribal site."

"It's not a tribal site."

"We don't know that. No one knows that. It could have been a tribal site. At one time *all* this land was tribal."

"Kate, experts can look at that stuff and tell where it came from. You won't be fooling anybody."

Kate angrily stuffed the cloth pouch into her bag

and got back up on her bike seat. "It just so happens, Brax, that these *were* found in Oregon. My parents have had them for years. I asked them to send them here. I told them it was for a project I'm working on."

Brax mounted his bike and pedaled fast to catch up.

"It would be a *lie*."

"Not necessarily!"

They reached the bridge and Kate dismounted silently. She leaned her bike up against the railing and headed down to the boulder.

When he reached the boulder, Kate was already perched in her favorite spot, watching for the beavers.

"Just think about it, ok?" she murmured. They were both getting used to talking in hushed tones.

"We could bury some old chicken bones and they'd think they'd discovered an ancient burial site..." Brax joked.

Kate ran her hands through her hair, pretending to ignore him. Then she looked at him and laughed.

"Shhhhh!" he hissed. They both looked toward the

den.

The beavers were swimming near the lodge. One baby rode on the mother's tail. The other swam next to her, playfully pushing his nose into her face.

Kate pulled out her phone and captured their family play in a video. As she reached over to hand the phone to Brax, they heard a noise neither had heard there before.

The sound of a high bark.

CHAPTER SIXTEEN

"That's not a dog."

Both Kate and Brax stood up. A clump of huckleberry bushes shivered near the water's edge. Brax put one finger to his lips and pointed toward the shrubs. Kate peered over his shoulder.

A red fox emerged from the center of the clump.

"Ohhhhhh…." Kate whispered. She lowered herself to the boulder and crawled on her hands and knees toward the backpack and the binoculars. Brax stood statue-like, transfixed by the fox.

Kate came back with the binoculars in hand. The fox was shuffling around the rocks near the river edge. He caught something from the water and chewed it vigorously.

"I've never seen a fox in the wild," Brax breathed. "It's so…cool."

Kate handed him the binoculars and took her phone from her pocket. She noiselessly recorded the fox searching, snapping, and chewing.

Suddenly she lowered her phone and rasped. "The beavers!"

They both looked toward the lodge, their eyes scanning the waters for their animal friends. The mother and her babies were gone.

"They must have seen the fox too."

Brax's tense shoulders dropped with relief. He didn't know if foxes and beavers were friends or enemies, or if they just left each other alone. He just knew he wanted his beavers to be *safe.*

The fox moved further downstream, darting in and out of bushes and occasionally nosing into the river.

"This place is *magical,*" Kate said reverently. "We have more than a summer adventure ahead of us...we have an important *mission.*"

She climbed up the boulder to the bridge and quickly mounted her bike.

"What are you doing?" Brax asked.

"We've got to find out where the developers will start digging first. We have to plant these artifacts before they get there!" Kate pedaled toward the trees.

"Kate, it's a crazy plan! It won't work, it *can't* work!" He scrambled to the bridge and leaped onto his bike.

"Well, we have to try!" She called over her shoulder. "We can't just do nothing!"

Brax pedaled fast to catch up. When he was just behind Kate he tried again.

"Let's think of something else. We can come up with another idea. We can think up a different plan!"

"No time, Brax. Unless you come up with a brilliant plan tonight, we have to get going on this." Kate pedaled faster.

Lying was wrong. That was what his parents always told him. But was it wrong if you lied to save someone? And would it be a lie, if like Kate said, the area was a tribal site anyway? If they did this no one could know about it. Ever.

Brax was good at keeping secrets.But now he had two: the beavers, and the plan to save them.

He poured on the speed. When he was within earshot of Kate, he called out to her.

"Do you know where we can get more of those

artifacts?!"

CHAPTER SEVENTEEN

Planting evidence was going to be a tricky business. Planting *false* evidence was going to be dangerous.

Brax had seen work crews excavating before. The big machines that knocked down trees and churned up soil didn't care what they ran over or destroyed. A small arrowhead or chunk of pottery could easily be overlooked. They'd have to place the artifacts somewhere sure of being discovered.

He didn't want anything to happen to his beavers. But he didn't want to go to jail either. If anyone found out that Kate and he had planted the artifacts, it could mean trouble for the rest of their lives. He didn't want to be known forever as a *liar*.

But dad says it's the intent that's important. He says if you lie to protect someone who's innocent, it means you have empathy.

He pulled up to the back door of his home. A lizard scampered across a large rock in the flower bed. Brax loved the chaotic style of their garden. Most of the people he knew had tidy backyards filled with mowed lawn and clipped hedges. But his backyard had a jungle quality to it. There were wildflowers, boulders, tall grasses, and even a small pond. His parents wanted animals to feel *comfortable* there.

He headed for the old concrete bench nestled among some overgrown bamboo plants. This was a private spot. A good thinking spot.

Brax was a thinker. He was good at thinking things through and making a decision and he watched other people carefully. He didn't want to make the same mistakes they did.

He snapped a piece of bamboo and stripped the leaves from the hollow stem. He tapped the woody tube on his knee as he thought.

The beavers need to be kept secret. I can trust Kate to keep the secret. Kate has a plan to keep the developers from digging up the old golf course land. But the plan involves a lie.

He blew air into the tube. The quiet, haunting sound made him relax.

A lie to protect the beavers is an unselfish lie.

But it's still a lie.

He beat the bamboo against the edge of the bench. The repetitive clicking sounded like a heartbeat.

If we aren't caught and the land is protected, we save the beavers and save ourselves. But if we're caught the evidence will be dismissed, the land will be torn up, and the beavers discovered. We could go to jail.

He tossed the bamboo tube into the weedy tangle of plants. Then he ran his hands through his hair and sighed.

Is a beaver's life more important than mine? Than Kate's?

"Brax?"

His mom was standing on the back porch.

"Yep." Brax came out of his woody thinking spot.

"Last day of school! Let's celebrate!" His mom gave him a warm hug and pulled him into the kitchen.

"Made your favorite," she said as she lifted a dish

towel from a steaming pan of lasagna. A chocolate layer cake sat on the center of the table. His mom was always looking for something to celebrate. To her, life was a party they were all invited to.

"This is a lot of food," she said. "Is there a friend you'd like to have over tonight?"

Brax had a lot on his mind. He didn't really feel like celebrating.

But he didn't want his mom to worry either. Or get suspicious.

He thought of the guys in the science club. He thought about his friends Micah and Brody. Those guys would really appreciate a meal like this. And he could talk to them about his biology presentation. Or about the summer science camp he was going to sign up for.

"Well?" his mom asked.

He leaned forward and smelled the steamy lasagna.

"Yeah. Kate."

CHAPTER EIGHTEEN

Brax used to imagine what he'd spend a million dollars on. If he *had* a million dollars.

Now he didn't care about a million dollars or even a hundred dollars. He cared more about the beavers, the river, the old bridge, and the secret he and Kate shared.

Kate pulled up to his house and leaned her bike against the garage door. He didn't even wait for her to knock before he rushed outside to warn her.

"My parents don't know about the beavers, so don't mention them."

"Oh." Kate smoothed her hair and adjusted her hoop earrings. "I'm glad you told me cuz I assumed you told them."

Brax fumbled with the screen door handle. "I figured I'd tell them sometime. But not yet. Just not yet." He held the door open for her. She brushed past him. Her hair smelled like strawberries.

His parents were already seated at the table,

reading current events on their phones.

"Welcome Kate." His dad pulled out a chair. "I know we haven't met before, but we've known your grandparents for quite a while."

Kate sat down. She pulled the white napkin off the table and laid it across her lap. "We don't visit my grandparents very much.... My parents are really into their careers. And *mine.*" She smiled.

"Brax tells us you're only here for the summer. He says you're going to do some modeling in California?" His mom scooped up some lasagna from the heavy dish.

"Yes, but not the whole summer. My parents are looking for a house in L.A. But I really like Beaver City." Kate gave Brax a smile.

"Well, tomorrow night is the town festival, why don't you come with us? It's to celebrate the beginning of summer!" His mom passed a basket of rolls to Kate.

Brax and his dad laughed.

"It's the town *beer* festival," Brax corrected her. "All

the parents drink beer to get ready for three months with their kids."

"Pssshhhhh!" His mom put her finger to her lips. They all laughed together.

"There are rides, booths, lots of food, musicians too," his dad volunteered. "We can all go together and you two can wander at will." Kate softly kicked Brax under the table. "Thank you, I'd love to!"

He knew what that kick meant. If they were free to wander at night, then they were free to sneak away and plant evidence.

"So…I was with my grandparents at the town meeting," Kate began. Brax kicked *her* under the table. "I know someone wants to develop the golf course land into housing. But what happens if there are special plants or animals that live there? What will the developers do then?"

Brax felt his palms begin to sweat and a flush of heat sweep over his head. *Why is she bringing this up?! She knows how important it is to keep this a secret. What is she up to?*

He tried his best to look mildly curious instead of showing the wild, angry panic he felt.

"Well, that is a problem," his mom responded. "Some developers will be careful about working around animal habitats and even restoring some of the land, but most of the time they're just thinking about the money."

"So, humans take precedence over animals." Kate lifted a forkful of cake to her mouth.

Brax was impressed. Most of the kids he knew didn't even know what *precedence* meant.

"Money speaks loudly," his dad chimed in. "Sometimes it shouts."

"There must be someone in Beaver City who knows its history really well," Kate said. "Maybe that person could help to protect the wildlife there." She looked innocently from face to face, then smiled and scooped up her last bite of cake.

She's trolling for information!

"Ms. Fontaine at the library is likely the most knowledgeable person in town when it comes to the history of Beaver City," his mom offered. "She was at the town meeting."

"She's also on the city council," his dad added. He cleared the dessert plates.

"The dinner was delicious. Thank you so much for inviting me." Kate dabbed at the corners of her mouth with her napkin. The gesture looked so graceful.

"It was lovely having you," his mom replied. "We'll see you tomorrow night!"

Brax had hardly tasted the lasagna or even the chocolate cake. But he didn't care. Kate had another plan. He needed to find out what it was.

He walked her out the front door. She swung her leg over her bike and paused. Brax lowered his voice.

"What are you up to?!"

"Who best to give us advice on where *artifacts might be found*! This Ms. Fontaine might be the insurance we need to get this done right." She adjusted her helmet and ran some lip gloss over her lips.

"So...you think we should go see Ms. Fontaine

before tomorrow night?"

"Machines are going to be digging up our beaver land. It's too easy for artifacts to be overlooked. Let's make sure we put them in the right place. Ms. Fontaine knows Beaver City better than anyone." She started pedaling.

Brax called after her. "At the library then? Right when it opens?"

"Yep!"

Suddenly tomorrow seemed years away. The town festival was just a night to celebrate the start of summer. But once he and Kate hid the relics, it might be the night that decided the future fate of the beavers.

And theirs.

CHAPTER NINETEEN

It was four in the morning and Brax couldn't sleep.

The library didn't open until eight and it would only take him 15 minutes to ride his bike there. He had a few hours to wait. And worry.

Adults were always saying worry was a waste of energy. His mom said that when he worried about a thing he had to go through the event *twice:* once when he worried about it and once when it happened.

But Brax knew worrying was useful. When he worried about a thing he could prepare for it, and decide how he was going to react.

Kate didn't seem worried. On the contrary, she seemed determined. But then, she was leaving Beaver City and could escape the consequences if this plan didn't work.

He really hadn't known Kate for very long, but now that they shared the beaver secret, it felt like they had always been friends.

He got up and went over to the window. A soft

breeze brought in the Beaver City smells he loved: pine and fir trees, the white roses in their front garden, and the damp, earthy scent that could only be found in rainy places like Oregon. A bat zipped past him at eye level, but he wasn't startled. He liked bats. They ate bugs. Annoying bugs like mosquitoes.

He nestled into the worn leather chair next to the window and pulled a blanket up to his chin. He watched the bat collect his evening meal. The next thing he knew, the sun was nudging him awake.

The clock said 7 a.m., just enough time to get ready and eat. But a knock on the door told him otherwise.

Kate had arrived early. She held her bike helmet in one hand and a white bag in the other.

She brought the artifacts with her? What was she thinking?!

Before he could lecture her, she opened the bag and put it near his nose. Donuts. Warm donuts.

"I love that little bakery on second street. The people who run it are so nice and it's open so early!"

Kate offered him the bag, then pulled one out for herself.

Brax pulled his bike from the side of the house and the two friends pedaled off to the library.

Ms. Fontaine was busy supervising the mass of young children who were there for the summer book fair and reading club. When Brax saw the chaos, his enthusiasm waned.

"There's no way she'll have time for us. Got any other ideas?"

Kate answered with her golden smile. She waded through the crowd and leaned in to Ms. Fontaine, raising the bag of donuts to nose level. Ms. Fontaine peered into the bag, then motioned to her assistant to take over. Kate made her way back to Brax with the librarian in tow.

"Are those from the Second Street bakery?" Ms. Fontaine reached into the open bag.

"Ms. Fontaine, you probably know Brax. My name is Kate. We need your help."

Don't do it. Don't bring her into the secret.

Ms. Fontaine polished off the donut and Kate offered her another.

"What can I do for you?"

"Brax and I went to the town meeting about those big developers wanting to build here in Beaver City. It seemed like a lot of people didn't want them to. We're curious about what happens next?"

Brax flushed red. Kate made it sound like they did *everything* together.

"Well, the city council will have to discuss it, make sure all the paperwork is legitimate and the proper studies have been done. If the council decides the development is in the best interests of the community, then an environmental survey team will research the proposed area and report back to us."

"A survey team?" Brax interjected.

"Yes, a team of environmentalists will study the land and any waterways connected to it. We've already commissioned them to begin." She took the last bite of donut and brushed her hands together. "They may find something that could put the project on hold."

"What would that 'something' be?" Kate scrunched up the empty donut bag.

"Oh, it could be any number of things. Endangered species, keystone species, whether or not the area holds a watershed, or even native artifacts of historic value."

"So, do these survey guys just choose any part of the land to study?" Brax steadied his voice to curb his excitement.

"No, no. We give them a study plan and they systematically comb through the entire area. We don't want a sample spot, we want to be thorough." Ms. Fontaine glanced at her assistant and the growing crowd of book lovers.

"So, they'll be starting at the north end of the old golf course?" Kate ventured.

"No, they're starting at the south-east end, right by that crop of big, granite boulders, and then moving north. I'm sorry. I really need to get back to the group. Did you need anything else?"

"No, that's it. Thank you, Ms. Fontaine." Kate smiled and tossed the crumpled bag into a nearby recycling bin. Ms. Fontaine hurried back to the group.

"That was slick, getting her to tell us where the surveyors will be."

Kate poked him. "Nobody says 'slick' anymore!"

Brax laughed.

CHAPTER TWENTY

Beer, beer, beer.

Everywhere Brax turned, he saw an adult with a beer in his or her hand. Perfect.

He and Kate would have no trouble sneaking off to plant the artifacts.

"Hey, project nerds, how's it going?!"

Lucas.

"Hey Lucas," Kate said politely. "How are you?"

"I'm fffffine…." Lucas faked a stagger toward them.

"You have apple cider in that cup, Lucas, you aren't fooling anyone." Brax tapped Kate on the arm. "Let's go."

Lucas straightened up and tossed the cup onto the ground. Kate glanced at the cup, then glared at Lucas. He sheepishly bent over and picked it up.

Oh the power of lip gloss. Brax rolled his eyes.

"Where's your posse, Lucas? It's not like you to hang out all alone."

Lucas gave a sly smile and nodded toward the

nearest carnival ride, where Gabe and Brandon were waiting in line.

"Well, it was nice seeing you." Kate turned to Brax. "Let's go get those *onion rings*."

Time to go.

The two friends weaved through the jovial crowd toward the back gate of the fairgrounds.

Before passing through the chain link gate they glanced around. People were everywhere but not one was looking their way. Brax held the gate open for Kate and they hurried away from the festival.

"Why doesn't Lucas like you?"

CHAPTER TWENTY-ONE

It was an honest question. He knew Kate wasn't trying to be rude, she really wanted to know. But it was a sensitive subject.

"When I was five years old I was on the same t-ball team as Lucas. One day the game was moving slow, I mean really slow. I was bored and I walked off the field. Lucas has been a brat about it ever since."

"But why should he care if you left the game? Who cares about that stuff when they're *five?*"

"Lucas is about winning. About being *the best.* If he doesn't win he gets really mad. Our team lost that day and I guess he thought it was my fault.." He kicked at a stone as they walked through a weedy field.

"So that's why he doesn't like you? Because of one t-ball game when you were five?

"Pretty much." He turned down the street that led toward his house.

"Let's use my bike, we can share. My

grandparents' house is closer and I can pedal faster than you." Kate laughed and pulled on his arm.

They crossed the street and started down a narrow alley. A small dog pounced out from behind a hedge and scampered toward them, barking shrilly. Brax laughed to himself. *Little dogs always bark so big.*

The dog ran right between them, heading for a tree behind Brax and Kate. As they watched, the dog circled the tree, growling and snarling.

"He must see a squirrel," Brax suggested. But Kate saw something else.

"That's not a squirrel. Someone's following us."

Brax squinted against the setting sun. There *was* a large form up in the tree, and a lower branch was shaking. Almost trembling.

Kate grabbed his arm and pulled him along faster. "Let the dog take care of it."

Brax pulled away from her grasp and turned in time to see the figure jump down from the tree and kick at the little dog.

Lucas!

"He's been following us!"

"*Thanks so much for walking me home, Brax, I really appreciate it!*" Kate marched up the wooden steps to her front porch. She smiled at Brax, winked, and walked in through the front door. As she slowly closed the door she pointed to the side yard and held up her phone.

Kate always has a back-up plan!

Brax waved and started walking away. He walked down the side yard of the house and darted quickly behind it. Kate sent him a text.

my bike is behind the trash cans -be out in 2.

From his hiding spot he could see Lucas darting from tree to shrub, then peering over a car parked in front of Kate's house.

What's he hoping to see? Why would he want to follow us? Is the festival that bad?

After a minute, he turned and headed back toward the festival.

He has the patience of a hamster.

A minute later Kate emerged with a handful of chocolate chip cookies.

"My parents never let me eat like this, but my grandma loves to bake." She gave him half the cookies. They were still warm.

"I'll pedal." Kate hopped on the bike and waited for him to climb on.

Brax sat behind her, his shoes hovering just above the pavement. He pointed to the top of the hill that led toward the old golf course.

"Don't be a back seat driver!" Kate laughed.

Brax laughed too. It felt good to let go of his worries and just enjoy the nighttime air as it whooshed past.

As they crested the hill, the sun dipped below the western trees, casting strange shadows across the grassy slope. The ground squirrels had been busy. New holes were everywhere. The pyramids of loose soil gave an eerie look to the hillside.

Kate angled the handlebars back and forth as she tried to circumvent the fresh mounds. She gave a yell just as she plowed through a mound and the tire plunged into a cavernous hole. The bicycle flipped. They flew.

Brax landed on his shoulder with a quick thud and rolled reflexively to one side. He jumped up and looked for Kate. She was sitting on a squirrel mound, brushing away tears with the back of her hand. He rushed over.

But she wasn't crying. She was laughing.

"Uh oh." He pointed to a cut on her face. "Looks like your modeling days are over."

Her laughter ended with a gasp as she fumbled in her pocket for a mirror. She pulled out a lip gloss tube with a tiny mirror on one side of the casing.

"You're kidding me, right?" Brax folded his arms in sarcastic disgust.

"Brax, I can't have a *scar*. That would totally be the end of *everything*!"

She sighed with relief as she lightly fingered the tiny scratch.

"I'm good, I'm good!" She swiped her lips with the

gloss and pocketed the case.

"Can we think about saving *beavers* now?" Brax picked up the bike and got on first. *"I'm driving."*

The two friends bumped along the dry, grassy field. The darkening sky urged them to hurry. When they reached the giant boulders, Brax skidded to a stop and they quickly dismounted.

Kate dropped her backpack to the ground. The wheat-like grasses waved in the evening breeze. Brax circled the massive stones, searching for the perfect planting spot.

"It can't be too obvious," Kate instructed. "It can't look intentional."

"Well, it can't sit on the top of the ground, or it will look like it was just dropped there," Brax countered. "But if we bury it, the digging will look too fresh."

"Oooooooo!" Kate teased. "Look who's thinking like an archeologist!"

Brax grinned in the dark. He stepped over some medium-sized stones nestled next to the massive rocks.

"What if we hollow out an area under some of these smaller stones and put the artifacts underneath? Then when they're discovered it will seem like the rocks slowly migrated over them. What do you think?"

"I think you're good at using vocabulary words we learned in English. But will anyone look under the rocks?"

"We'll leave an arrowhead half buried nearby. Once they see that, the surveyors will search the whole area."

"I like it." Kate pulled the artifacts from her pack.

A coyote gave a mournful howl as the two friends lifted the rocks. The nocturnal world was just waking up. Kate pulled a flashlight from her pack and shined the light around them. A bat skimmed the air above. The frogs near the river's edge started up their night-time chorus. Brax smoothed the soil around the rocks and kicked the dirt up to give it a more natural surface. He backed up and looked at their work.

The rocks and soil looked guilty, like a fresh crime.

Kate seemed to read his thoughts. "It will look better in the daylight. C'mon, let's head back before it gets too late."

Brax checked his phone. They had plenty of time to ride back before the festival ended. He swung his leg onto the bike and waited for Kate to get on the back.

That was easy.

Too easy.

CHAPTER TWENTY-TWO

Evidence hid. Development delayed. Beavers saved.

...Possibly.

Brax lay in bed that night rolling from side to side, staring at the wall, then staring out the window.

They'd just saved the beavers. He should feel like a hero.

So why didn't he?

Even if it worked and the developers had to give up, would he still have that nagging feeling that he'd cheated? Was this a secret he would have to hold on to forever? And if he or Kate did tell, would that put the beavers back into the line of fire? Ms. Fontaine said a discovery of artifacts could *delay* the developers. She never said it would stop them forever.

Brax had nightmares that night. Images of huge boulders rolling at him, giant beavers the size of dinosaurs, and Ms. Fontaine eating so many donuts that she grew enormous and popped like an overblown balloon. Ridiculous and disturbing.

"It's so nice that you and Kate are friends," his mother said at breakfast the next morning. "It's hard to move from one school to another. I'm glad you're helping her feel welcome."

His dad shifted in his seat and put down his coffee. "The town website says the environmental team is going to inspect the old golf course soon. Maybe today."

His mom put another muffin on Brax's plate and stroked the top of his head, the way she always did, as if he were still a little kid. Or a puppy.

"What would you guys say to a day trip? Let's get the canoe out and paddle down the river for a bit. Do you think Kate would like to come?" She sat down across from Brax and picked up the coffee pot.

Brax snorted.

"What's funny?" his mom stopped pouring.

He tried to imagine Kate in a canoe. She was a city kid, not a canoeing kid.

"That sounds great to me," his dad chimed in. "I'll

get the canoe ready."

His parents were always ready for an outdoor adventure.

Then again, a canoe trip might be just what he needed to stop thinking about the planted artifacts— and the imminent inspection.

"Fine. But I doubt she's ever held a paddle in her entire life."

"She can sit in the middle on the spare canvas seat we have," his mom offered. "We can stop by that organic bistro on the way home for some lunch!"

Brax finished his juice and sent Kate a text. She replied right away.

I'd love to come!

He was excited to show Kate the world he loved. Seeing wildlife from a canoe was even better than walking through a field or a wood. In a canoe you could glide along, nearly invisible, observing every creature.

And of course, she'd see how skilled he was at canoeing. How well he knew the river. How quickly he could recognize the animals there. She'd see he was strong and smart even though he didn't do team sports.

He was right: Kate had never paddled before. She'd never even been in a canoe. When she stepped in and the boat wobbled back and forth, she grabbed the sides in a panic. He tried not to laugh.

"You'll get used to that feeling," his dad reassured her. "By the end of the morning you won't even notice the sway."

Brax glanced at Kate to see if she was watching him. He had his own paddle. He dipped it in the smooth water, ran his hand along the side of the boat, then gave his wrist a slight flick before pulling the paddle out. The 'J' stroke was easy for him.

The river was quiet. No one else was out this early. A flock of ducks socialized on the river bank, preening their glossy wing feathers and nibbling at the green grasses poking out of the mud. As the canoe approached, one duck glanced up with a curious eye before returning to its preening. Kate looked like she wanted to stretch out her arm and touch one of the ducks. But she didn't.

"Mallards," Brax said in a low voice. He pointed to a line of six babies bobbing behind their momma in the water. Where she went they went.

They turned the canoe and headed down a curved section of river. The grasses were taller here and a great blue heron stood statue-like at the river's edge. When the canoe was within a few yards, the bird spread its gray wings and lifted into the air without a sound. Kate wordlessly watched it fly up into a massive oak tree, her eyes wide with wonder.

As they glided through the calm flow, small turtles flipped from their warm rocks into the protective waters. Frogs resting on lily pads plopped under the river's surface. Fish flicked their tails as they tried to capture an early morning meal of gnats and mayflies. It was a familiar and comfortable world to Brax. But he knew it was a whole new world to Kate.

A ribbon of fog snaked through the trees near the river bank and a deer poked its nose from behind a tall shrub. When it saw the canoe, it stopped in its tracks.

Brax smiled. "That deer thinks if it holds very still we won't see it."

"It's beautiful," was all Kate said.

The morning soon melted away and the sun rose steadily into the sky. When it was directly over their heads, Brax's mom started planning.

"Let's head on back to the launch for *lunch*." She laughed at herself. Brax rolled his eyes.

Paddling back upstream against the current took more work. Brax tried to make it look effortless, but his occasional grunts betrayed him. When the canoe was safely secured to the top of the truck, Kate finally spoke.

Thanks for inviting me, it was so fun!"

"Anytime!" his parents said simultaneously.

Later that afternoon, the truck pulled up to Kate's grandparents' home. Brax jumped out to walk her up to the door.

"I don't think you worried once about your hair," he teased.

"I know…." Kate sighed happily. "Wasn't it great?"

CHAPTER TWENTY-THREE

"You are not going to believe this!"

Brax had just woken and come down the stairs to breakfast. His dad was reading from a tablet propped in front of the coffee pot.

"Believe what?" Brax rubbed his eyes sleepily.

Native American artifacts were discovered on the old golf course parcel! They are being studied for authenticity."

Brax was pretty sure he must be dreaming… There was no way their plan could have worked so well. And so fast! They couldn't have been that lucky...could they?

"Isn't it great?" His mom put a dish of steel-cut oats on the table in front of him, along with a small jug of fresh cream.

But it was hard to eat with his heart pounding and his palms sweating.

"What kind of stuff did they find?" He sat down and stirred some cream into his bowl.

"The article doesn't say," his dad answered. "But it must have been significant. The city council has called an emergency meeting to put a hold on the development project."

Brax scooped up a large spoonful of oats and stared at it. He couldn't swallow right now if his life depended on it.

"It says here that an expert is being flown in from Seattle to examine whatever it is they found. Pretty exciting news for Beaver City." His dad sipped at his coffee and looked up.

"You ok, Brax? You love oats and cream!"

Brax realized he'd been holding the same spoonful near his mouth without moving for several seconds. He wasn't sure what he felt. He needed to talk to Kate.

"Too many corn dogs last night," he lied.

There it was. His first lie to his parents. Brax felt a guilty flush sweep over his face and neck.

His mom reached into the refrigerator and pulled out a small bottle of blackberry drinking vinegar. She was always coming up with some 'natural' cure for whatever ailed him. He looked at the bottle as she poured the contents into a glass.

Why can't she just use antacids like everyone else?

Brax took the glass of vinegar and got up from the table.

"I'll drink this in my room. I think I'll lay down for a while."

He snatched his phone from the charging cradle and hurried up the stairs. It was tempting to pour the glass out the window, but he wasn't going to lie to his parents again. Pinching his nose he drank the vinegar quickly to keep his word, then sent Kate a text.

Did you read the news yet?

He paced the floor. He looked out the window. He flopped on his bed. Then a text came in.

It happened! Just like we wanted!

Now what? He texted back.

Let's celebrate! was the enthusiastic reply.

And do what?

There was a long pause. Then something hit his window. He rushed over to see Kate standing next to her bike, laughing. He opened the window and she answered him.

"Let's go spend a day with our beavers!"

CHAPTER TWENTY-FOUR

"I brought us some crullers," Kate said. She held up a white paper bag.

"We're going *fishing?*" Brax pulled his bike up next to hers.

"Fishing? What are you talking about?"

"You said you brought some *crawlers.* Crawlers are used to catch fish."

Kate laughed. Her laugh seemed different today. Sunnier. More carefree.

She pulled a pastry from the bag and handed it to Brax. "Crullers from the bakery."

"These are donuts," he countered.

"Well, whatever they are, they're really good." She bit into one.

As they rode along the alleyway, Brax shouted out a question: "How come you always have money for 'crawlers'? Are your grandparents rich?"

"My grandparents aren't rich. I'm just an only child. They like giving me spending money."

"I'm an only child too, but I don't get 'crawler' money."

"Yes, but I'm *pampered.*" She was leaving him in her dust. He pedaled faster.

They crested the dry grassy hill and paused before heading down.

"Watch for the squirrel holes this time," Brax said.

They started down and expertly swerved around the dirt mounds. They were getting to know the hill.

The path to the beavers used to seem long:.. the hill, the field, the woods, the open space, and the bridge. Now the ride was shorter. Familiar.

They both knew the protocol. Hushed voices once the bridge was in view. No speaking on the bridge. Only whispering allowed on the rock. Phones on silent. Binoculars always.

Kate asked him once about dangling their feet in the river, but he remembered all too well his own experience slipping off the rock. So he brought a rope from the garage, tied it to the stone bridge post, and let it hang over the rail. If she wanted to dangle, she had to tie herself to the bridge first. So did he, for that matter. It was simply protocol.

Kate reached for the rope and tied herself securely. Then she inched her way to the bottom of the rock and into the water.

"Hey…." Brax began.

"Don't worry! I'm only going in up to my knees."

They were silent, scanning the river for signs of beaver activity.

"So, we planted the artifacts. What now?" Brax whispered.

"We wait and see. And enjoy our success!"

The mother beaver emerged from the underwater doorway, the two babies following. They were growing quickly.

The beaver dam had carved out a quiet pond from the boisterous river. The babies swam safely in this watery playground with the dam there to protect them. Their mother rarely ventured into the stream flow. She must have known her babies would follow.

"Yesterday was a really great day," Kate

whispered.

Brax nodded. He picked up the binoculars and followed the beavers.

"You're really strong, Brax. And confident. It's like the river is your friend."

Brax didn't respond. He kept searching the water.

"To me, nature has always felt like a stranger. A little scary."

He kept the lenses at his eyes. "Makes sense, you live in a different world."

"I always liked my world. Now I'm not sure."

Brax pointed at one of the babies who was slapping its tail in the water. The other swam over to join in the game. It was hard not to laugh as they watched the baby beavers slap the water--and occasionally each other.

"Maybe we should name them," Kate suggested.

"Well...they don't belong to us. Not really."

He looked up into the thick tree canopy. Spots of blue sky framed the dark black birds flitting among the branches.

Kate scooted up the rock and untied the rope.

"You know Brax, you're just as strong as any of the guys on the football team.."

"I do like sports, I just don't want to go to all those practices and games. It's too much."

"Like my life!" Kate nearly forgot to whisper.

"Exactly! We should get to be kids without having our whole lives planned for us all the time!"

"You have no idea…." Kate's eyes misted over.

They watched the baby beavers push and pull at floating sticks like a game of catch.

Kate moved closer to him. She leaned her head on his shoulder and breathed out a heavy sigh.

The two babies followed their mother to the far end of the pond. When she picked up a large stick in her teeth, they mimicked her. They followed her back to the lodge and added their sticks to the growing mound.

"Looks like playtime is over," Brax noted.

"Even beavers grow up," Kate sighed.

CHAPTER TWENTY-FIVE

The artifacts turned out to be authentic Native American pieces.

Brax had been so busy visiting the beavers with Kate, he nearly forgot about the specialist.

They'd spent nearly every day there over the past week, sitting on their favorite rock. He showed her how to tie knots: bowline, two half hitches, square knot, taut-line hitch. He taught her how to find huckleberries, blackberries, and salmon berries in the woods.

In return, she shared the photo editing apps on her phone. They captured dozens of photos of their time in the woods.

They talked about everything they saw: raccoons, woodpeckers, the silver-gray moss on the oak trees. They sat silently for hours and watched the baby beavers play while their mama kept a careful eye on her offspring.

On Monday, Kate brought their lunch in her

backpack and they ate sandwiches on the stone bridge above the river. On Tuesday, Brax made a small fire pit from river rocks and they roasted sausages on long tree branches he had whittled smooth.

On Friday, Kate received an email from her parents. They had found a house and would return to Oregon for her in two weeks.

"Two weeks?" Brax felt the cold shock of the news. He always knew Kate wouldn't stay in Beaver City forever, but he had lost track of time. The weeks had melted into one long summer day.

"My grandparents said there's another town meeting next week, on Monday. The city council will hear what the community wants to do next." Kate dipped her feet in the river, the rope tied securely around her waist. It was easier to talk about the town meeting than about her going away.

"What has the city council said so far?" Brax was crafting a makeshift fishing pole from a tree branch and some cotton string.

"The council is thinking of having a huge area dug up to look for more artifacts." Kate smiled weakly.

He pulled the pole back, then flung the string-line over his head and into the stream. The salmon berry he had tied to the end bobbed on the water before vanishing under the surface.

They were both silent for a few minutes. Finally Brax spoke.

"Do you feel as weird about this whole thing as I do?"

Kate smoothed her long braid and looked at her reflection in the water. He hadn't seen her do that in a while.

"*You* wanted to save the beavers," she retorted. "This was the only idea I could come up with!"

"*We* wanted to save the beavers." He pulled his line up empty.

"Hmmmmm." She fumbled through her bag for a comb, unbraided her hair, combed through it, and started the braid over.

"We're going to the town meeting, right?" Brax

dissembled the pole and string and tossed the tree branch down into the water.

"Definitely."

Suddenly he felt restless. The beavers slid under the surface and headed for their lodge. Kate fiddled with her hair. He jumped to his feet and climbed up the rock toward the bridge.

"C'mon, let's go."

Brax pulled his bike away from Kate's and got on. He didn't want to be with her right now. He didn't want to watch for the beavers. He needed to be in his thinking spot in his backyard. He needed to be alone.

The ride back was silent. When they reached the alley behind Kate's house, Brax kept peddling. "See you later," he called over his shoulder.

"You OK, Brax?" Kate pulled her bike to the side of the garage. He didn't answer. Instead, he turned the corner and rode on down the street toward home.

Kate was leaving.

CHAPTER TWENTY-SIX

He wished he hadn't met her.

Before she came, things were fine. He had summer science camp and his friends Micah and Brody. He enjoyed canoeing with his parents and riding his bike to the old golf course. He had a million dollar beaver secret. Then Kate came.

Nothing was simple anymore.

He'd shared his million dollar secret with her. He'd lied to his parents. He'd planted false evidence and deceived the *whole town.* Now he had a secret he'd have to keep forever.

And now he had a best friend named Kate. A best friend who was leaving in two weeks.

He put his bike in the garage and headed up to his room. No thinking spot today, he'd already done enough thinking. He raced up the stairs, plopped on his bed and kicked off his shoes. Angry tears pooled in his eyes.

He jumped up and walked to the window. A cool

breeze rustled through his hair.

Beaver City looked different to him now. He could never go back to the way things were before Kate.

Are you mad at me?

It was a text from Kate.

No. I'll see you at the town meeting.

It was all he could think to say.

There was a whole weekend until the town meeting, but he couldn't think of anything he wanted to do. He curled up in the worn chair. The leather squeaked as he nestled in and pulled his favorite blanket around him. Then he did something he hadn't done in a long time. He buried his face in the old blanket and cried.

CHAPTER TWENTY-SEVEN

A cool fog settled over Beaver City the morning of the town meeting, shrouding the hills and ground with a gray fuzziness. By evening the fog would burn off, but for now it reflected exactly how he felt: unclear.

Kate had come into his life and now she would leave. It was simple, really. But it didn't feel simple. He hadn't even known her very long, but he felt like they had always been friends.

She was a friend he could be himself with. If he felt quiet and serious, she was OK with that. If he wanted to be loud and ridiculous, she was OK with that, too. She never made fun of him. She was someone he could *trust.*

His thoughts clouded over. He really didn't know that much about Kate. Not really. Sitting in the chair by his window, he tried to think of everything he knew about her: where was she born? What's her favorite color? What are her parents' names?

How can you trust someone you hardly know?

He got up and walked over to his desk where all his treasures sat. He poked at the bird nest he and Kate found on one of their visits to the lodge. He picked up the smooth stone she'd given him as a totem. She said it had the power to settle jumbled thoughts when he held it in his hand. He knew she made that up, but he didn't care. He held the stone in the palm of his hand and squeezed it tight.

When he thought about Kate leaving, a hot lump burned in his chest. He looked around his room at all the artifacts of their brief friendship. He thought of their heroic plan to save the beavers.

She may be leaving but she hasn't left yet. We still need to secure a safe life for the beavers.

He started to return the stone to his desk, then dropped it into his pocket instead. He picked up his phone and saw. several texts from Kate.

The doorbell rang. He went down to answer it.

"I did warn you," Kate held up her phone.

"Yeah…I slept in."

"We've never gone to see the beavers in the fog,"

she began. "It would be fun to see if we can get there in one piece!" Her backpack slipped off her shoulder and hit the floor with a heavy thud.

"What's in there?" Brax reached over to pick up the pack.

"Lunch and a great idea." She zipped open the pack and pulled out a small canister. "I saw this cool video on the internet where you can make plaster casts of things. I thought we could search for some paw prints of our beavers and make plaster paws!" Her eyes sparkled with enthusiasm.

Clever. And creative. Brax felt his brain-fog lift.

The gray swirled around their bicycle pedals like earthy dust. Everything looked different in the fog. Even familiar landmarks popped up out of the mist with a ghostly surprise. Kate was right, this was a great idea.

Navigating the stony hill in the fog, with its squirrel mounds, was now very dangerous. Brax was surprised how much Kate was enjoying the ride. She tried to jump over the mounds instead of going around them and she laughed each time she nearly fell. No one would guess that this girl was preparing for a career in modeling.

They both made it to the bottom of the hill with only a near-miss. Pedaling through the field and seeing the evergreen trees poke out of the heavy sky felt like entering a new world.

The bridge emerged before them like a slice of an ancient castle. The surface was slippery from the damp moss. They parked their bikes and headed for the rock.

"Let's see if the beavers are out," Kate suggested. "Then we can find their paw prints and make some casts."

The rock was damp from the fog rising off the water. They sat at the top and she pulled out the binoculars.

The mother beaver was already pulling long grasses from the riverbank with her strong claws and packing away the greens with her rusty teeth. The two babies crouched on either side of her, chewing at the reedy plants. The mother climbed up the riverbank and picked up a downed branch, then hauled it back into the water. With the branch in her mouth and her babies flanking her, she headed back toward the den.

"Perfect!" Kate exclaimed. She tugged at his arm and climbed up over the bridge railing. "Footprints!"

"You mean 'paw prints'." His sadness was lifting like the rising mist. The two of them carefully picked their way through the shrubs and berry bushes to where the beavers had been.

"Couldn't be better," Kate declared as she bent down, carefully clearing away the leaves and debris to reveal clear paw prints of both mother and babies.

Brax held the canister of plaster mix and read the instructions. "Just add water, stir, pour on the spot, let it dry."

"This is going to look so cool!"

They always spoke quietly here, but even so, he could hear the excitement in her voice. While they waited for the plaster to dry, he scoped out a grassy clearing where they could eat their lunch. Whatever

Kate had brought would be good.

"Dessert first!" She pulled out two baked half-circles of puffy dough and handed him one.

"What is it."

Kate's honey laugh was muffled in the foggy woods. "Hand pies. My grandmother makes them. These are made from the blackberries you and I picked."

The pies were still warm.

"My grandmother says hand pies were invented a long time ago, for field workers to carry with them for lunch. No forks needed!"

The pie tasted like summer. Like *this* summer.

She pulled out two bottles of lemonade. Then she revealed the main course: bread balls

"What exactly is this?" Brax scrunched his face.

"I promise it's really good! It's a bread bowl sandwich. My grandma's specialty." She lifted the lid of the bread bowl and peered inside. "Avocados, cheese, hummus, sprouts, tomatoes...all in an edible bowl!"

"My mom would *love* this," Brax laughed.

The two friends ate in silence as the fog lifted into the summer sky.

CHAPTER TWENTY-EIGHT

The community center was packed with people. The early morning fog left the air outside cool and clean, but the room smelled of old damp wood.

This time Brax sat with Kate. He didn't care what Lucas thought, and he didn't care what his friends thought either. He didn't even worry about thinking up an excuse to tell the science club.

The city council talked about the artifacts and about putting the development project on hold until more research could be done. The council and the developers argued about contracts, expectations, and something called 'civic duty'.

Kate scrolled through her phone, showing him the best photos she had edited. They laughed and they remembered. He was happy. The beavers were safe, it had been a great day, and he and Kate were best friends. For the moment, he wasn't going to think about her leaving.

The man who represented the developers pulled

out some maps of the old golf course. Brax nudged Kate. "Let's go see."

They squeezed through the crowd of people gathered around the table. When they got close enough, Brax saw a bright red circle around the area where the artifacts were discovered. He felt a flush of heat rush to his face.

Such an important decision, all based on a lie. Our lie.

He just wanted to save the beavers, to keep his million-dollar secret. He never wanted to start a war. But that was what it felt like now: everyone arguing and taking sides.

Some argued that construction would ruin the wildlife area and put the animals' lives at risk. Others said the space was needed for housing and the jobs it would create. The words swirled around him and the shouting pounded in his ears. He wanted to run from the guilt.

Kate must have felt it too. She grabbed his hand and led him back to their seats. But the chair where she'd left her phone was empty. The phone was gone. They heard a familiar laugh.

Lucas.

"Nice pics, cute little couple," he sneered as he scrolled through the photos. Kate snatched her phone back.

"Lucas! I can't believe you would look through my phone!" She was livid. "Don't you know anything about boundaries, about privacy?!"

It wasn't just an angry statement, it was a real question. She stood still, waiting for the answer.

Lucas turned red. Really red. His face was blotchy and flushed. He opened his mouth to answer but nothing came out. Kate waited.

"It's because he thinks he's better than everyone else," Brax quietly answered. "He thinks just because he's good at *one thing*, that makes him good at everything, but it doesn't." He pulled at Kate's arm. "Let's go."

Outside, the air was cooling and the sky glowed night-time red. The two friends walked across the parking lot toward Kate's house. Suddenly, she stopped.

"What is it?"

She didn't answer. Instead, she held the phone up. He looked at the photo on the screen.

It was a picture of the beavers and their den, with the bridge railing in front.

Kate's voice shook. "He knows."

CHAPTER TWENTY-NINE

The beavers now faced a whole new kind of danger: Lucas.

"He knows," Kate repeated. "Soon, they'll all know! Lucas, Gabe, Brandon…they won't leave this alone!" Panic rose in her voice.

"We can't do anything about it tonight," Brax said. "And neither can they. They might not even figure out where those photos were taken." He tried to sound comforting, but he knew Kate was right. If Lucas found out where the den was, he wouldn't leave it alone.

"What if they tell other people? Beavers in Beaver City…." Kate began pacing back and forth. "What if they make the connection to the artifacts?!"

"C'mon, they aren't that smart." His hollow laugh sounded forced.

"We have to go first thing in the morning. Do you think your parents will let you go that early?"

"Sure. They trust me, and they really like you. I

think they'll be ok with it."

"We'll leave at seven," Kate pronounced. She turned down the alley and headed for her grandparents' house.

It was a long night.

He wanted to sleep. He wasn't tired, but he wanted the night to pass quickly so he could go check on the beavers. His thoughts shifted between the beavers and the development. Each time he started to doze off, he'd jerk awake suddenly.

He looked at his bedside clock. It was 2 a.m.

Lucas won't figure it out. I've never seen him hanging out near the old golf course. He'll tease us for a while, then forget about it.

Anyway, Lucas was nearly always at football or baseball or basketball practice. He wouldn't care about the woods. Then a new thought came to him.

If Lucas realized there hadn't been a beaver in Beaver City for so long, and he saw the beavers in the photos, he'd surely tell someone. He'd want the credit of the *discovery* to be his own.

When he rolled over to look at the clock again, it was 6:50 a.m. Kate would be there soon.

He quietly dressed and put his phone in his pocket, then tiptoed down the stairs. His parents had approved his early morning adventure to "see the sunrise," but there was no point in waking them up, even so.

Kate was there, one foot poised on a pedal, eager to go.

"Did you sleep much?" she asked.

"No. You?"

She shook her head.

The two rode in silence. After navigating the squirrel hill, Brax spoke.

"I doubt Lucas even noticed the beavers. Or he might have thought they were just pictures of beavers from anywhere. Not ones we took. We weren't in the photo."

Kate nodded but pedaled faster.

"Those could be beavers from Montana, or Colorado!" He was out of breath from the speedy ride and trying to talk. Kate kept pedaling.

When they reached the woods, they heard an unfamiliar sound. It carried up from the river and out through the dense trees. It wasn't the rush of water or the snap of falling branches. It wasn't the cry of the fox or the chatter of birds. The sound echoed through the area, bouncing off boulders and weaving through the evergreens.

The sound of human voices.

CHAPTER THIRTY

Brax sped ahead of Kate. When he reached the bridge, he jumped off and dropped his bike hard. He grabbed the edge of the stone bridge and leaned over.

Lucas was standing at the river's edge, laughing. Brandon was crushing the top of the beaver den with heavy stones while Gabe jumped up and down on the dam, pulling branches from the weave.

Kate forgot the quiet rule and yelled as loud as she could.

"Lucas!"

In one bound, Brax swung his legs over the bridge and landed on the boulder below. He slid down the mossy rock and leaped to the riverbank, wordlessly marched over to Brandon, pulled the stone from his hands, and shoved him to the ground.

"Leave it alone, Brandon!" He looked over at the beaver den. It was already partly dismantled, and the roof was smashed in. Loose sticks and twigs were steadily streaming down the river. He scanned the riverbanks, but he didn't see the beavers.

"They must be inside!" Kate yelled. She climbed over the bridge and shimmied down the boulder, then waded through a narrow section of the waters' flow to get a better view. When she saw the damage up close, she gasped.

"Nooooooo!" She wailed mournfully. Then she turned toward the boys. "How could you do it?!"

The question echoed down the river. As if in response, the dam gave a low moan. The remaining logs and branches creaked and gave way to the stream.

In one heavy crash, the dam burst apart.

The water rushed downstream, pulling the dam and the den with it.

Gabe went too.

Brandon jumped to his feet. "He can't swim!"

Gabe's arms flailed and splashed as he screamed.

Meanwhile, the massive pile of tree limbs became a deadly tangle. The mound that had protected the beavers all summer disintegrated in the water's rush downstream.

Lucas turned to Brax. "What do we do?!"

Brax looked downstream ahead of Gabe, searching for the answer.

"Hurry Brax! Do something!" Kate screamed desperately.

All eyes focused on Brax. Gabe's screams morphed into choking sounds as the river dragged him further downstream.

Brax couldn't think. No totem could help him now. There wasn't time to make a plan. He looked up at Kate and jumped into the river.

He quickly spotted a sturdy log and swam for it.

With one arm holding the log he paddled hard with his free arm and kicked furiously with his legs. He had to catch up with Gabe before he hit the culvert up ahead.

Brax knew that if Gabe reached the culvert grill, the pressure would trap him there, crush him, and drag him under.

Gabe was bobbing under the water and then surfacing, up and down like a cork. With each gulp of air, he screamed and gurgled, desperately trying to stay afloat.

Brax steered the log with his whole body. He had to guide Gabe away from the culvert.

He was only feet away but it felt like miles. He almost reached out a hand to Gabe, but he couldn't risk letting go of the log. Not yet.

He inched his way to the end of the log and kicked hard. Gabe was just an arm's length away.

Then he remembered something his dad had told him.

Always approach a panicked swimmer from behind. A drowning person won't think clearly. They'll grab you and try to get above the water, pushing you under.

He ducked beneath the surface and swam under the log. When he emerged, he was right at the back of Gabe's head. Holding tightly to the log, he stretched his free arm around Gabe's neck.

"I'm here, Gabe, it's Brax! It's going to be OK!"

Gabe clutched at his arm with both hands while Brax pulled him toward the log.

"Grab the log!" Brax commanded.

Obediently, Gabe released his grip and grasped the log with all his might. With both hands free, Brax pushed the log, arms stretched to full length, toward the riverbank where Lucas stood holding out a long branch.

"Grab it! Grab it!" Both Lucas and Kate were shouting.

Gabe's wide eyes and pale skin revealed his exhaustion, but he let go of the log and snatched at the extended branch. Lucas and Kate pulled him to shore, dragging him up through the weedy grass and over the slippery stones.

With a final push of energy, Brax paddled the log closer to shore.

Then he heard Kate scream.

CHAPTER THIRTY-ONE

The last pile of logs from the dam hit Brax from behind and pushed him further out into the river.

His back stung from the blow, and the shock forced the air from his lungs.

The angry mass dragged him toward the deadly culvert.

When he was little, he used to wonder what it would be like to be something other than what he was. *An eagle that could fly higher than almost any other bird. A deer that could leap over a cliff and run down the side of a mountain.*

Right now, he wished he was a beaver. A beaver with a huge rudder-like tail and swimming claws. He'd paddle swiftly to shore. A beaver was at ease in the water. A beaver would survive this.

Just before swirling down into the culvert, the river took a sudden bend to the right of the giant pipe. Brax looked up and saw a willow tree leaning protectively over the water. Its branches hovered just above the roaring surface. The tree reached out to him, offering one last chance to escape a watery death. With a deep breath, he lunged with both hands.

The wispy branches looked feeble, but they were strong and wiry. He grabbed the largest clump he could wrap his hands around, but he didn't know how long he could hold on.

The river pulled at him hungrily. A sudden wave in the current forced him around to face the riverbank.

Most people who drown are facing the land when they die.

CHAPTER THIRTY-TWO

Brax was pretty sure he'd been in the water for a long time because he was hallucinating. He saw both his parents standing on the bank. His mom was tying one end of a rope to a large oak tree and his dad was tying the other end around his waist. He wore a bright orange life vest.

The color of beaver teeth.

Then his dad was swimming toward him, his powerful strokes mastering the river's force.

He felt his dad's strong arm wrap around him. He was too scared to let go of the willow tree, and even if he wanted to, his hands were locked on to the twisty branches.

"Let go, Brax!" his dad shouted.

"I can't! My hands won't let go!"

A flash of movement caught his eye. Kate joined his mom near the river's edge. She grabbed the rope and held it firm.

His dad lowered his voice. He spoke calmly. The

sound lifted above the roiling stream.

"I've got you Brax. Let go of the tree."

Brax exhaled the breath he had thought might be his last. He let the willow branches slip from his hands. His dad swam them back to shore.

CHAPTER THIRTY-THREE

Brax was angry. Really angry.

After the destruction of the dam and the near drowning of both himself and Gabe, the whole town knew about the beavers. And Brax was pretty sure he knew who told them.

His mom had confined him to the house for a day or two. Not as a punishment, but as a precaution. She watched him vigilantly for signs of 'secondary drowning,' or drowning due to water left over in the lungs. Even though he assured her he hadn't swallowed or inhaled any water, she kept watching him.

This confinement gave him time to think. To sort.

And to feel really angry.

He pulled out the totem from his pocket. Miraculously, the rock had survived the river ordeal. He sat on his bed clutching the cool stone in his hand.

He was mad at Lucas for being Lucas.

Stupid, selfish Lucas.

He was mad at Brandon and Gabe for destroying the dam and the den.

Gabe and I almost didn't grow up.

And he was mad at Kate.

She'd moved here and weasled her way into the beaver secret. She'd left her phone on the chair, where Lucas found it and saw the beaver photos.

She was leaving soon. Her parents were here for a brief stay in Beaver City before they all left for their new home.

She must have guessed how Brax felt. She hadn't texted him at all for the past two days. On his first day of freedom, she sent a short message.

Want to go see if the beavers are ok?

His phone had survived the river ordeal too, but now he threw it on his desk.

Do I want to see if the beavers are ok?! How could the beavers be ok?!

Their home, their entire environment, was destroyed!

He looked out his bedroom window. It was a cool,

sunny morning. A family of chickadees called to each other from the cherry trees.

How can they be so happy with everything that's happening?!

His mom knocked on the door and came in.

"Dr. Philip says you're good to go. I know you want to hang with Kate, but no going near the river, understood?"

He forced a smile.

"Kate's here." His mom ruffled his hair and picked up an empty plate from his desk.

Kate was sitting at the kitchen table. She had brought the usual white bag with her.

"For a girl who's going to be a model, you eat a lot of donuts." Anger punctuated his words.

"I really don't want to be a model, and you know that," Kate retorted. "How are you feeling?"

It annoyed him how thoughtful she was. He wanted to have more reasons to stay angry with her.

Then it won't hurt so much when she leaves.

When they walked out the front door, Kate got

right to the point.

"We *have* to go check on the beavers."

"I'm not supposed to go near the river."

"*Near* is a very unclear term. We can check on them from the bridge without going *near* the water." She pulled her bike from behind the garage wall and waited.

He was angry. But he was curious. And worried.

"Fine." He yanked his bike from the garage with one frustrated pull.

They traveled the familiar path in silence. Brax wondered what they would see at the river. Would people be there? Would the area be taped off? Would the beavers be gone?

When they neared the bridge, they cautiously slowed down. No people were there. No yellow tape.

No beaver dam or lodge.

The dam had washed downstream in a heap and the den was a hollowed out mound. They both leaned over the bridge railing to get a closer look.

Kate moaned.

On the shore was one of the baby beavers.

It was dead.

Frantically, they scanned the area.

No other beavers.

"They're all dead." Brax forced the words.

The two friends sat down on the bridge. Neither one spoke. The river kept tumbling by, oblivious of the death on its banks.

Brax stood up and walked to the edge of the bridge with his back to Kate. Then his anger burst like the broken dam.

"Why did you leave your phone on the seat?! Who does that?! Who just leaves their phone out for anyone to look at?!" Tears burned in his eyes.

"Are you saying…."

"If you hadn't moved here, none of this would have happened! I had a secret…a million dollar secret!" He was sobbing now.

"This isn't my fault! It's all because of those selfish, immature boys!" Kate was crying too.

She reached for her bike and mounted it angrily.

He could hear her crying as she pedaled off the bridge and through the woods.

He took the totem from his pocket and squeezed it tightly in his fist. Then he hurled the stone into the water. The ripples traveled out and hit the walls of the ruined, vacant den. Brax dragged his tired feet toward the muddy bank and the stone steps he had created ages ago. He plodded down the steps, then waded through the shallow, narrow rivulet that bordered the larger stream.

He reached the baby beaver and hovered over it. His tears dropped carelessly on the carcass. Then he bent down and stroked the beaver's coat.

A beaver summer, he bitterly thought.

He lifted the beaver and carried it to the stream. He wanted to bury it, to give the animal a proper resting place. But he didn't want a fox or a coyote to dig it up. Better to return the beaver to its natural home. The river.

He crouched down and carefully laid the beaver on the surface of the water. The small body bobbed rhythmically, quietly, then joined the stream's flow. He watched the water carry the beaver as far as he could see. With slumped shoulders, he waded back to the stone steps.

The secret wasn't a secret anymore, but it didn't matter now. The beavers were gone, and Kate was leaving.

I never want to come back here. Not ever.

CHAPTER THIRTY-FOUR

"Hey, did you see this?" His dad held up his tablet. "More artifacts were found in that same spot. Turns out those initial findings weren't some random sample from a native tribe. They're uncovering evidence of an entire village settlement. Amazing!"

"You're kidding." Brax plunked into a kitchen chair with a dead thud.

His dad slid the tablet across the table.

Brax grunted bitterly. "Figures."

He got up from the table and clumped up the stairs. Kate's plan had worked better than either of them ever suspected. There really were artifacts to stop the development and protect the beavers.

But now it was too late.

In his room, he picked up his phone. He wanted to text Kate, to talk to her about it all. But after what he'd said to her, he didn't expect she would speak to him again. *Ever.*

And he couldn't blame her.

He flopped on his bed and stared at the ceiling. He'd really made a mess of things. Shared his beaver secret. Lied with Kate. Deceived his parents. Started a town war. And worst of all: the beavers were dead.

A huge mess.

His phone clicked.

Good news! Looks like the old golf course will be safe after all!

Kate.

A shower of pebbles hit his window. He darted down the stairs and out the front door.

"We may not have been able to save the beavers," Kate almost whispered. "But the rest of the wildlife there will thank us." She smiled weakly.

She was right. They'd been so caught up in worrying about the beavers, they never thought about the other animals that needed protection.

"My parents say we're leaving tomorrow. Do you want to make one last visit to the river?"

Brax felt his anger and bitterness fade as he watched Kate get on her bike and adjust her backpack. His promise to never return to the old bridge faded too.

When they reached the top of squirrel hill, Kate paused.

"You do realize that not only did you stand up to Lucas, you saved Gabe's life. That makes you the town hero right now."

"*We* saved Gabe's life," he corrected her. They started down the hill.

Their bikes bumped along the rocky field. Kate tore ahead as usual, but then she slowed to let him catch up.

"We made a huge discovery for Beaver City," she said. "Do you think we should tell anyone? Or should it always be a secret?"

They peddled side by side. He looked over and smiled at her, but didn't answer.

Just before they reached the old bridge, he got off his bike and walked it the rest of the way. The place seemed solemn somehow, like a cemetery. Kate dismounted and followed him quietly through the trees.

Much of the moss had withered in the summer heat, giving the old bridge a different face. The water was lower now. The tumbling river that had nearly claimed his life passed calmly under the bridge. One week of warm weather had changed everything.

Brax stopped just short of the bridge. He gazed at all the rugged beauty around him. He heard the noisy chatter of the birds. He smelled the hot weedy scent of the summer heat on the river grass. A squirrel scampered up an oak tree. Twigs snapped in the undergrowth.

"Are you afraid we might see the others dead too?" Kate pulled her bike to a stop.

"No. I wasn't thinking about that." Brax stared straight ahead into the woods. "Kate…." he began. "You're the best friend I've ever had."

"And you're the best friend I've ever had."

"I'm so *sad* that you're leaving." he articulated.

She took a deep breath. "California and that *new life* seem a world away. I like *this* life." She pushed her bike onto the bridge and leaned it against the rails.

Brax wiped his eyes. He looked at her face.

"I hear there are great theme parks there, and lots of sandy beaches."

"And diets and clothing and photo sessions and making sure I look perfect."

"Yeah, you've kind of let yourself go." He flicked her long braid.

She leaned over the bridge, trying to see her reflection. He laughed. The wind quietly rustled the trees.

Kate turned to him. "I'm so sorry about the beavers."

Brax watched a bird flitting in the trees, chirping happily.

In a perfect world everyone would care about the beavers. This isn't that world.

"It's not your fault. It's not my fault either. We did our best to help save them, to save this whole area. There wasn't much we could do. After all, we're just kids."

"*Sneaky* kids!" She laughed her golden, honey laugh.

He leaned against the bridge rail and peered down at the river. He didn't see any dead beavers. He turned back to Kate.

"How did you get into modeling?"

"I told you before...I was born cute. *Really* cute. My parents didn't want that to go to waste."

"Did they ever ask what you wanted to do?"

She shrugged. "No one decided anything, really. It just kind of happened. I was so young then, I don't remember, anyway."

"Do you think they'll ever ask you?" .

"Like you said, we're kids. We don't get to decide much. My parents have invested *big time* in this future career for me. They've spent years getting me ready for this. They've found new jobs and a new place to live. It's really important to them." Kate fiddled with her hair nervously.

"What's important to you?" Brax straightened up.

159

"Getting good grades in school, being a good daughter to my parents." The words sounded scripted, like lines from a play.

"Yes, but what do you really care about? What do you want?"

"Look Brax, not all of us get parents who let us roam the woods and canoe rivers and study birds!" She let out a frustrated sigh.

"Are you saying I'm *spoiled*?"

"No. I'm saying you're *lucky*. We all get what we get."

She picked up a small stone from the bridge. He watched as she leaned over and tossed it into the stream.

Brax thought about his parents. His house. Growing up in Beaver City. He thought about his friends. His freedom. His explorations.

I have a good life.

"People would say that *you're* lucky," he told her. "You're smart, good with computers, pretty, and really nice to people."

She smiled. Her eyes watered.

"We'll have to text every day, and you can send me pictures of California. I'll send you pictures of Beaver City. It will be like you never left! I'll even send you some donuts!"

Kate rubbed her eyes and laughed.

"And when you're famous and I see you on the cover of a magazine in a grocery store, I'll say: that girl is my best friend."

"*If* that ever happens, Brax, you won't just see it in a grocery store. I'll send you an autographed copy!"

Kate pulled out her phone. Together, they scrolled through the many photos of their summer together. There were the beavers, happily playing together in the water. There were the plaster prints they had made of their paws. There was the den, healthy and whole, and the dam holding the water back, creating a wildlife paradise.

There were funny photos of the two of them, and beautiful photos of the forest creatures. A northern flicker, a gray tree squirrel, a chickadee, a fox. All captured forever.

"Let's get a picture of us on our last summer day together," Kate suggested.

Brax stood with his back against the concrete rails of the bridge. Kate leaned in next to him. They made faces as she snapped each image.

"Last one. Let's make this serious." Kate raised her arm way above her head, trying to include the river behind them. She snapped the photo.

"Let's see."

He held his hand above the phone to shade the dappled sunlight coming through the trees.

"We look good!" Kate laughed.

He took the phone from her. He squinted at the screen. He walked to the end of the bridge into the shade.

"Come see this..."

He zoomed in on the photo. There it was! Something behind them. Kate peered over his shoulder.

"What is that?" she said the words slowly, as if

afraid of the answer.

Brax rushed back to the middle of the bridge. He leaned against the rails.

"Do you have the binoculars?"

She pulled out the lenses from her backpack so quickly, she nearly dropped them.

He first focused one lens and then the other. When the view was balanced, he squinted hard. Then he turned and handed the lenses to Kate.

"No, I don't want to look."

"Yeah, you do."

"No more sadness." She backed away.

"Just look."

With a sniff, she put the lenses up to her eyes. Brax put his hands on her shoulders and turned her toward the river.

"Do you see it?"

There, where the river bent near the willow tree, a flurry of activity stirred the water. A mound of sticks lay in a straight line, diverting the river. There they were: a large animal with a smaller one, busily dragging sticks to the top of the mound.

She lowered the lenses and smiled at him.

Brax grinned.

"Beavers."

The End

Literature Circle Questions:

1. Why do boys tease Brax? Do you get teased? What do you get teased about? Why do you think people tease you?

2. Brax gets bullied by someone at school but he doesn't tell anyone about it. Why doesn't he tell? Should he?

3. Brax says he has a million dollar secret. Who does he decide to share the secret with? Why?

4. Brax believes a cell phone is too personal of an item to take to school, or any public place. Why does he feel this way? Do you agree?

5. Kate's parents have decided her future for her. Do parents have the right to do this? Do parents always know what's best for their children? What do children owe to their parents?

6. Brax says he feels more lonely at school than when he is alone in nature. Why do you think he feels this way? Have you ever felt alone in a crowd of people?

7. Brax tells a lie. Why do people lie? Is there ever a good reason to lie?

8. Kate and Brax deceive the whole town. How do they do this? Is it a good thing?

9. Is a person's life worth risking to save an animal's? What do you think determines the value of life, either human or animal?

10. Brax and Kate talk about being "lucky." Kate also says "we get what we get." How does luck play a part in their lives? How does luck play a part in yours?

Literature Activities:

1. Native American artifacts tell great stories. Visit a museum that has these artifacts or go online and search for some.

2. Kate gives Brax a totem to help him unjumble his thoughts. Keep a journal for a week to help you unjumble your own thoughts.

3. Brax throws a stone in the river and watches the ripples spread. Find a smooth stone, throw it in a body of water, and see how far the ripples extend out. Think about how the choices you make ripple out to affect other people.